For Liz Cross. Who else?

OXFORD
UNIVERSITY PRESS

Great Clarendon Street, Oxford OX2 6DP

Oxford University Press is a department of the University of Oxford.
It furthers the University's objective of excellence in research, scholarship,
and education by publishing worldwide. Oxford is a registered trade mark of
Oxford University Press in the UK and in certain other countries

British Library Cataloguing in Publication Data
Data available

ISBN: 978-0-19-274999-4

1 3 5 7 9 10 8 6 4 2

Printed in India

Paper used in the production of this book is a natural,
recyclable product made from wood grown in sustainable forests.
The manufacturing process conforms to the environmental
regulations of the country of origin.

ALI SPARKES

NIGHT FOREVER

OXFORD
UNIVERSITY PRESS

Elena felt something inside her simply collapse with terror. She couldn't do this. She couldn't. She couldn't.

'It's OK,' called a small, quavering voice. Tima was attempting a smile as she hung over an incomprehensible drop. 'Just do what he says. It's easy . . . really.'

'Put your feet flat against the spire,' said Hazza. 'And lean back against the ropes. Put your feet wide . . . make a triangle. Don't look down.'

Stepping over the edge nearly burst her heart. She thought she might faint and her limbs seemed to dissolve with panic. All she could do was stare, terrified, into the steady brown eyes of the man who was pushing her off the Burj Khalifa. He's an expert. He's an expert. He's an expert, she chanted to herself. He knows what he's doing. You're safe.

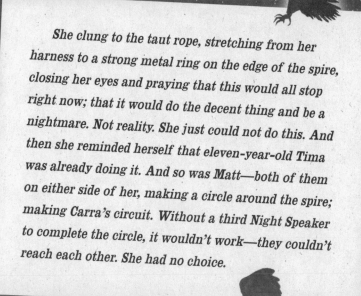

She clung to the taut rope, stretching from her harness to a strong metal ring on the edge of the spire, closing her eyes and praying that this would all stop right now; that it would do the decent thing and be a nightmare. Not reality. She just could not do this. And then she reminded herself that eleven-year-old Tima was already doing it. And so was Matt—both of them on either side of her, making a circle around the spire; making Carra's circuit. Without a third Night Speaker to complete the circle, it wouldn't work—they couldn't reach each other. She had no choice.

CHAPTER 1

We shouldn't be here.

As the bridge filled up with early morning spectators, the knot in the pit of Elena's belly grew tighter.

We really shouldn't be here.

'Come on, everyone, move along and find a space.' Mr Cochrane, his reflective yellow tabard gleaming in the dawn sun, was waving twenty students and two teaching assistants along to lean over the stone wall of the ancient river crossing. Most of the students were looking unimpressed. They'd been promised a natural wonder but all they could see on this cold April morning was a sluggish river with muddy banks.

'Oh god—we SHOULDN'T BE HERE!'

It was only when Mr Cochrane and several of the nearest students turned to stare at her that Elena realized her last urgent inner cry had actually been an urgent *outer* cry. She'd *shouted* it.

'What's the problem, Elena?' asked Mr Cochrane, glancing at her briefly before fixing his eyes back on the north-eastern horizon where the river seemed to dissolve into the flat green land.

Elena grappled for the words. How could she ever explain this?

'Sir . . . I . . . I don't think it's safe. Where we are right now.'

Mr Cochrane didn't unpin his gaze from the furthest reaches of the river. 'Sssssssh, everyone,' he called out. 'We might be able to hear it coming.'

The students fell silent and Elena, every part of her skin awash with goosebumps, peered at the side of the geography teacher's head in desperation. 'Sir . . . ?'

'You're perfectly safe, Elena,' he said. 'The Wiggenhall Wave is only a metre above the usual river depth. It's not a tsunami.'

Elena turned to stare north-east, along with everyone else. Of course it wasn't a tsunami. It was just the Wiggenhall Wave. A minor natural phenomenon. Every so often high tides out in The Wash would overwhelm the outflow of the River Great Ouse and send a bore wave back up it for several miles. The funnel shape of the river valley meant the wave rose up quite impressively—sometimes people even surfed on it.

But it was a small wave. That was all.

'It should be visible in the next thirty seconds or so,' said Mr Cochrane, consulting his watch and a printout of the tide timetables. 'It'll be worth getting up so early for, trust me!'

Elena could already see a small wave. Not in the river but

along its banks. Voles, mice, and rats were heading up through the grass, a miniature tsunami of mammals making for higher ground. Couldn't anyone else SEE this?

'SIR! We have to GET OFF THIS BRIDGE!' She actually grabbed his arm this time and he turned to stare at her, affronted. At that moment the sound of distant sirens rose in the air, along with a low rumble on the horizon.

'I'm not messing around!' Elena heard the panic in her voice. 'We're not SAFE here!'

'Sir . . .' said one of the other students. 'What's that?'

'It's the bore,' said Mr Cochrane, wrenching his arm away from Elena and turning back to the river. 'And it's perfectly *what the hell?!*'

'RUN!' Elena yelled, sprinting for the far side. 'EVERYONE! *NOW!*'

But they just stared, dumbfounded, at the grey mass on the horizon and the creatures fleeing the riverbank and even the birds now swooping overhead with shrieks of alarm.

Mr Cochrane finally lifted his loud teachery voice and said: 'Everybody—I think we might need to—'

'RUUUUUUN!' screamed Elena.

At *last* they seemed to understand. The wall of grey water was clearly visible now. Some of the kids screamed, picking up the panic, *finally* feeling the threat. They ran after her as she raced across the bridge, heading for the higher ground of the high street. Glancing back she saw that about a third, on the far side of the bridge, were stumbling away in the other direction. The rest seemed to be milling about in shocked uncertainty while their teacher just stood, rigidly gripping the bridge wall and gaping at the unthinkable scene before him.

'SIR! *MOVE!*' bellowed Elena, and maybe he finally believed his own ears and eyes because the bore was now tearing up the river, gaining height with every passing second. It should have been only a metre higher than the usual river surface. It was at least *four* metres higher. Finally, Mr Cochrane bellowed: 'RUN!' and began to shove the remaining two students ahead of him, aiming for Elena's side of the bridge.

It was too late. They hadn't reached the nearest parapet before the tidal bore surged over them, smashing across the bridge wall like a stampede of foaming grey horses. The force was immense. It picked them up like dolls, along with its cargo of broken branches, old tyres, metal panels, and at least one dead animal—a calf, Elena's mind flashed, regretfully. The teacher and students were washed over the far side and into the river where the rest of the bore tore on relentlessly. They didn't even have time to scream.

Displaced river was washing around her knees and threatening to topple her but Elena managed to wade across and spot the yellow tabards as they spun and bobbed in the current, travelling at speed. 'PLEASE!' she screamed. 'PLEASE! HELP THEM!'

She didn't know whether she'd got through—didn't know if it was even possible for her friends to help. There were only a few of them here, safe in their holts ... was it even fair to ask? They could be swept away too ...

But they were expert swimmers and right now, they were

literally the only hope. Shutting out the shrieking and wailing from her classmates and the panicky shouts of Wiggenhall locals as floodwaters abruptly shattered the peace of breakfast, she closed her eyes and sent her plea again. *HELP THEM! PLEASE! They can't survive this!*

And just before the yellow tabards were lost from view she saw the first sleek dark figure emerge from the flooded bank and flip over into the water.

Two more followed, one of them glancing back at her for a microsecond as it battled the boiling wake of the bore.

Thank you! she sent. She had no idea whether it would make any difference now, but if three strong otters couldn't catch up with Mr Cochrane and the others and save them, nobody else could.

As the flood drained away her fellow students clung to each other, shocked and confused, while the teaching assistants, with shrill, shaking voices, tried to do a headcount. Elena clambered onto the bridge wall and sat there, shivering. Fresh sirens had started up, coming from the west. Most of the village had probably dialled 999.

Jessie Cheam staggered up to her, trying to speak through panicky sobs. 'What happened?' she spluttered. 'What *was* that?'

'It was the wave,' said Elena in a voice much calmer than she felt. 'It was just much bigger than we thought.'

'How did you know?' Jessie scrubbed the tears off her face, trying to get herself under control.

'I just . . . got a feeling,' said Elena.

Jessie nodded slowly and stared upstream. The water was still angry but settling behind the bore wave, which was now out of sight. 'Are they dead?' she said.

'I don't think so,' said Elena. 'I think . . . they might get out alive.'

'Who was it?'

'Mr Cochrane and Dan Spelman and—I think—Megan Vasili.' Elena gulped. Putting names to the students made this nightmare more real.

'Megan can't swim,' whispered Jessie.

CHAPTER 2

'Matteus Tomasz Wheeler, please stand.'

Matt stood up. He did his best to keep his breathing slow and steady. He did not want to look as if he was about to cry.

A dark flicker in the high window at the back of the courtroom caught his eye and for a second he felt comforted. It was as if she'd come to remind him that everything he'd done, he'd done for the best; for a good reason.

'Matteus,' said the magistrate, 'you have already pleaded guilty to the charge of taking a vehicle without consent and driving without a valid licence or insurance.' She sighed and took off her spectacles, fixing him with a long stare. 'Since your arrest in December, I appreciate that this trial has taken a very long time to come around, thanks to backlog issues with the CPS which are none of your doing. You have no doubt experienced a great deal of anxiety about coming to court today, and had several months to consider your actions. Joyriding up and down the country in a stolen car is not acceptable behaviour in a 15-year-old in any circumstance—but it's certainly made worse when the 15-year-old in question has stolen the car from his own father's valeting business.'

Matt couldn't help glancing up at Dad. His father sat in the public gallery in his best suit, staring straight ahead as if he'd been chiselled from stone. Mum sat beside him, focusing on the floor; he suspected she too was trying not to cry.

'You put your family's business reputation on the line, as well as your own safety, when you chose to take that car,' the magistrate went on. 'This makes me very seriously consider a custodial sentence, even though this is your first offence.'

She paused, allowing her words to sink in. Matt bunched up his fists and felt sweat trickle between his shoulder blades. His best shirt was sticking to him under his suit jacket. The flicker in the window couldn't stop his heart rate increasing. Was he about to be sent to a young offenders' institution? The social worker had said it was very unlikely . . . but not impossible.

'Before I pass sentence,' said the magistrate, 'do you have anything that you'd like to say? You've chosen to remain silent so far, but it is still possible for you to make a statement in your defence; to explain *why* you did this. Right now is your last chance to do that, Matteus.'

Matteus stood up straight, held up his hand, and allowed the starling hovering at the open window to fly down and land on it. 'I really am sorry, Your Worship,' he said, 'to put my mum and dad through so much worry. I didn't ever mean to do that. And I would never have borrowed the car if it hadn't been a matter of life and death. You see, I knew a friend was in desperate danger and I had to get to her quickly. Only, if I'd tried to explain to anyone that I'd been told this by two golden eagles, in the middle of the night in Norfolk, nobody would have believed me. I didn't have time to explain and I couldn't afford to pay for a taxi. So I took the car. I always meant to return it and replace the fuel; in fact, I was replacing the fuel when the police arrested me. Also . . . if I hadn't done it, most of the Scottish Highlands would have collapsed into a massive crater by now. If you don't believe me, ask my starling friend.'

'Massive crater,' said Lucky, on his fist. 'Believe.'

Imagine if he *had* said that.

Yeah, right.

Matteus chose not to speak. Instead he just gazed solemnly at his knuckles and waited.

The magistrate sighed and put her glasses back on. 'Matteus Thomasz Wheeler,' she said. 'I have considered sentencing you to a four month detention and training order . . . however in the light of your age and your admission of guilt I am willing to give you a chance to make amends. Therefore I am imposing a referral order with our youth offending team, for your rehabilitation. This means that you will carry out some reparation in the community. You will need to sign a contract, along with your parents, to commit to certain standards of behaviour, and to carrying out tasks that are beneficial to the people of Thornleigh.'

Matt nodded, still reeling from the first part of her
sentence—*detention*—and now blinking at the crashing relief of
the second part—*referral order*.

'You will arrive at the right time, in the right place,' Her
Worship went on, 'and perform whatever task is put before
you to the best of your ability, without complaint, while under
supervision. Failure to do this will land you back in court. And
if I see your name come up again I will reserve your case to deal
with myself.' She eyed him with a steely glare. 'I won't be so
lenient next time, Matteus.'

'Yes, Your Worship,' he mumbled.

She nodded, closed a file and concluded: 'Your parents will
cover court costs of £85. The detail of your reparation duties will
be explained to you before you leave today. I hope this is the last
time I see you in my court, Matteus.'

'Thank you.' Matt turned and walked down the steps into
the subterranean corridor of the courthouse, led by a remand
officer, Mum following close behind. The duty solicitor had
departed some time ago. In refusing to speak about his reasons
for taking the Land Rover he'd also given the man very little to
do, other than state that he was a first time offender who had
pleaded guilty at once. There was nothing anyone could say in
his defence if he himself wouldn't say a word about it beyond: 'I
just did it because I wanted to.'

He felt paper in his pocket and smiled for the first time in
what felt like weeks. It was a handwritten note from Elena and
Tima, his best friends, and the only people in Thornleigh who

knew exactly why he'd become a car thief.

We'll be thinking of you today, Elena had written, in her neat handwriting. *Whatever happens, remember that you were amazing. You did what you had to do. We will always be here for you. ALWAYS.*

Underneath Elena had signed her name with one x and so had Tima. Tima, being theatrical, had drawn a heart around her x. The letter had arrived that morning, flown through the window in Lucky's beak. Since Dad had permanently removed his mobile phone, Luckymail was the only way he could get quick messages to his friends—and get them back again. Sometimes it was a note and sometimes the starling would just repeat what Elena or Tima had said to her. Her dark rainbow-feathered throat would vibrate and she would somehow produce an eerie recording of one of them, sounding just the same, only a bit higher in pitch. It was beyond weird to hear Lucky say: 'Hi Matt—see you at the hide tonight, usual time.' She didn't really do very long messages—they tended to get a bit mangled, so that's when the notes had started. Matt did not know how he would have survived the past few months without his carrier starling.

It took another hour to go through all the paperwork with Mum at his side, signing his promise to attend his meetings and his duties, which seemed to be mostly litter picking. In fact, Matt was in no hurry to leave. He would happily have spent all day in the Youth Offending Team office if he could have avoided his father.

As soon as it was all over the remand officer showed them back out into the corridor, where Mum threw her arms around him. 'It's such good news!' she breathed. 'SUCH good news.'

Then they had to leave the court and meet Dad.

Dad was poking a cigarette butt around with one shoe. He glanced up as they emerged from the side door of the courts and Matt really thought, in that moment, that his father would have preferred it if he *had* gone to jail. And maybe that was the truth because spending time with Dad had been almost unbearable since the day he'd come to bail him out after his arrest last December. On that cold winter's morning they'd driven home in seething silence but as soon as they'd parked outside Kowski Kar Klean, Dad had dragged him out of the car, slammed him up against the wall of the car wash and hit him across the face.

And then Matt had done something he'd never done before, despite years of slaps and shoves and beatings. He'd hit his dad back, right on the jaw. It wasn't that hard a punch; Matt had been exhausted—but his father was shocked into silence. A look flashed across his puffy features that might almost have been fear.

And then, instead of pummelling his son into the brickwork, he'd just said: 'Inside. You've got a lot of explaining to do.'

He was wrong about that. Matt wasn't going to explain. It was out of the question. From that day to this, he'd not explained anything. He'd only said: 'I took the car. I just wanted to.'

He had also said: 'I always meant to bring it back.' And

that was it. Not even Mum could get anything out of him. Explanations were simply not an option because NOBODY was ever going to believe what he said . . . and if they did . . .

Matt glanced up and saw Lucky roosting on the high gabled roof of Thornleigh Magistrates' Court as they walked down the stone steps in the April sun. He could only imagine what might happen to Lucky if the truth about their telepathic connection ever came out. Questions, capture, experiments . . .

It was ironic that, just as soon as he'd stopped being a surly, closed-down, troublesome teenager, he'd had to start *pretending* to be a surly, closed-down, troublesome teenager. It was the only convincing thing he could do. If it kept Lucky safe, it was worth it.

As soon as they got home from court Matt went to his room to get out of his suit (bought especially for his court appearance) and into his jeans and T-shirt, while Mum made him a cup of tea. He grabbed a piece of lightweight paper (he'd bought an old style airmail notepad so his messages wouldn't be too weighty) and scribbled a message to Elena and Tima.

It's OK. Not going to jail. See you tonight.

Lucky was already waiting on the windowsill. She snapped the message up in her pale yellow beak and took flight immediately. Matt let out a long sigh. Tonight he would wake up at 1.34 a.m. when the beam came through his bedroom, and then meet Elena and Tima in the hide, in the woods. They would sit around the little paraffin heater, drink hot chocolate from Elena's flask, talk about his court appearance . . . and then put it all behind them.

Maybe this was the point when things *finally* got better. Maybe now he could get his life back on track; start to think about a future. He only had another year to go at school and then he could maybe get away from Kowski Kar Klean and his dad. He could join the Navy like Ben, his big brother. Or . . . something. Matt rested his head against the window, pondering. Since becoming a Night Speaker, everything had changed. For years he'd planned to run away to the Navy at sixteen but things were different now. There was Lucky, for a start.

He dreamed of working with animals these days. It was the obvious career for someone with his talents; if you could talk directly to birds and other creatures and have them talk right back to you, why wouldn't you want to work with them? He could be a big success at a zoo or wildlife sanctuary or maybe one of those places that specialized in birds. He'd have to cover up his Night Speaker powers, somehow—he wouldn't want to start freaking people out—but he'd find a way.

Only . . . you couldn't run away to a zoo or a wildlife sanctuary at 16. You would probably have to go to college and get at least an A Level in biology or something. Or just do lots of volunteering until you got a job out of it. Which would all be fine if he didn't have to stay *here*, at home with Dad, while he did it. One day soon, things were going to get too bad for him to stay; he knew it.

He shook his head. He would talk to Elena and Tima about it tonight. Maybe they'd have some good ideas.

A high-pitched, buzzing whine broke through his thoughts. Matt blinked, put down his pen and the notepaper, and wandered out of his room. He found Dad at the front door of the flat, with an electric screwdriver. Mum leant in the doorway of the kitchen, her face tight and pale, her arms folded across her chest.

'What's going on?' asked Matt, tension rising in him once again.

'What does it look like?' said Dad.

Matt moved closer and peered over his father's shoulder. A gleaming metal clasp was affixed to the wall beside the door and Dad was attaching another one to the door itself. It was a thick, heavy-duty thing; he'd seen something like it on outbuildings and warehouses . . . but on the outside.

Dad finished and put the electric screwdriver down. He picked up a massive padlock from the carpet, coupled up the two clasp rings and hooked the padlock through.

'What *is* this?' asked Matt.

Dad got up, shooting him a blank look, and clicked the padlock shut. He took the key out of it and put it deep into his jeans pocket.

'You might have escaped jail today,' he said, 'but that doesn't mean you're going to carry on as normal. You're not going to start sneaking out at nights and stealing cars again. I've seen to it. You stay *home* every night. You go to school, you come home, you do some cars, get your homework done, you get your food, and you get to bed. That's it.'

'You're padlocking me in at night?' Matt gaped at his father.

'Seriously?'

Dad jabbed him hard in the centre of his chest. 'You're lucky I'm not putting this on your bedroom door,' he said. 'And if you didn't need to pee, I would.'

Matt felt rage rising through him. He clenched his fists and took a deep breath. It was only Mum watching that stopped him jabbing his dad right back again. 'It's OK, Dad,' he said, through gritted teeth, his voice cold and steady. 'You've only got another year to go and then I'll be gone, just as soon as I'm sixteen.'

'You can't go *anywhere* without my say so, sixteen or not,' said Dad, glaring at him. 'You're in *my* charge until you're eighteen.'

'I'll sign up for the Navy,' said Matt. 'I won't let you stop me.'

'Please . . . both of you!' Mum cut in. 'It's been a hard day. A hard time. We mustn't fight. Come on . . . I've made tea.'

'I'm not fighting,' said Matt. 'I'm just making plans.' And he turned and went back into his room before anyone could say anything else.

Lucky got back five minutes later with a message from Tima.

Brilliant news! See you tonight!

Matt stared at the long drop from his window ledge. He grabbed Tima's bit of paper and scrawled on the back:

Yeah, well . . . about that.

CHAPTER 3

The best time to be a vampire was definitely full moon. Anyone taking on the role will tell you that lighting is *everything*.

When Spin stepped out of his basement he was bathed in a silvery glow. It rippled across the black silk of his trench coat and gave the red lining lowlights of purple. Best of all, moonlight behind him gave him a fabulous silhouette—and lit his white blond hair like a halo. Which was *hilarious* irony.

It was good that he was enjoying it all again. Truth be told, he'd gone off the whole vampire thing for a few months over the winter. He'd been a bit ... well ... there was no other word for it ... depressed. It made him prickle with embarrassment to think of it. Vampires didn't get *depressed*. Not even vampires like him.

But weirdly, the spring, with its longer, brighter days, had seemed to wake some optimism in him. Maybe it was just because there were more potential victims out at night, now it wasn't so cold. He had worked on his fitness and was now back to his old self and ready to terrorize the nightlife of Thornleigh once more.

Only, he was probably going to stay away from the woods beyond Leigh Hill, and the bandstand . . . and certain streets. There was some nightlife he *didn't* want to meet. It was too wearying.

Turning resolutely away from these locations, Spin began to sprint along the dim streets of his domain; soft-soled black boots almost silent on the tarmac and stone. It was just past midnight, on a week night—there wouldn't be many people about to see him and if they did, he'd be little more than a dark blur. He went east, to the back streets of the rougher end of town, where a pleasing overlook waited for him to ascend and brood. It was a derelict 1930s cinema, halfway along a shabby street filled with takeaways and charity shops. The out of control Virginia creeper along its side access made a perfect climbing wall up to the flat roof behind the crumbling plaster façade.

Some developer would surely be dribbling to turn it into an Art Deco block of flats, but happily for Spin, there was not even a For Sale sign on it. He climbed the creeper and arrived on the roof in less than a minute. The surface was covered in sticky, perished black pitch and occasional sprouts of scrawny buddleia. It was worryingly spongy in places; Spin kept to the edges. He had, some time ago, brought up a wooden crate and placed it next to a hexagonal glassless window in the façade wall. Here he could sit, unnoticed, and watch the town's late-night passers-by . . .

passing by. Nobody ever looked up.

Across the road from the old cinema was a pub—the Lock Keeper's Arms. It was past closing but a few stragglers were still smoking and burbling drunkenly at each other along its front wall. Maybe he'd take whoever was last to go home. He tried to work up an appetite for his odd brand of fun and games . . . but couldn't quite locate the urge. Maybe it was the cloud of midges hanging in the air around him, distracting him.

In truth, Spin hadn't found a victim in a while. He was more picky about it these days. Actually . . . he hadn't found a victim *at all*. Sometimes he wondered if he was losing the desire. Maybe he'd had enough of other people's fear.

But no. It was fine. He was still Spin. He was still *he who should not be named*. He was still . . . 'Oh, give it a rest,' he told himself. 'Admit it. It's just not the same without them.'

After a moment, he got up, stepped away, and turned to argue . . . as if his shadow self was still waiting on the crate. 'You don't *need* them. They were only a distraction. They messed you up.'

Sitting down again, he answered: 'Yes, Spin. But we both know the best times you ever had were when you were getting messed up by Night Speakers. You miss it. You miss the messing.'

'Shhhhhh,' he hissed back at himself. 'Somebody will hear you talking like a MAD PERSON.'

He lapsed into silence and let his eyes rest on the street below, brooding. Sometimes he could make himself so still even *he* wasn't sure he was actually breathing. It was a kind of meditation. It made him acutely aware of any other living, breathing thing in the dark.

So when he sensed movement behind him, his reaction was instant. He turned a somersault through the air, his coat billowing out behind him like wings, while setting off a dense, powdery cloud of smoke.

Then he swept out a leg in a semicircle and sent his stalker over—splat—onto the roof.

It was only when he heard the squeak that he realized, with a stab of shock, who it was. He'd been about to vanish but instead he stood up, wafted away some of the smoke, and stared down at the small figure at his feet.

'For crying out loud, Spin,' she choked. 'You've got to stop smoking!'

'*Tima?*' He knelt down and shone one of his pencil-thin lights into her face. 'What the hell are *you* doing up here?'

A small, dark-haired girl with flashing brown eyes and a very angry mouth glared back at him. 'Looking for *you*, you idiot!'

Spin sat down, cross-legged, and raised an eyebrow. 'And how did you *find* me? This isn't your usual territory.'

Tima pointed to the cloud of midges, now quite dense above them and making a spiralling shape.

'Ah, your little bloodsucking friends helped, I see,' said Spin.

'Takes one to know one,' said Tima. 'Or have you given up the whole vampire thing these days?'

Spin wafted a bit of red lining and slid out a pair of upper fangs. 'Are you offering?'

Tima rolled her eyes. 'Seriously?'

'No,' he said, with a sigh. 'You're way too young. What are you these days . . . eight? Nine?'

'I'm *eleven*—nearly *twelve*,' she snapped. 'And you know it. I'm just small for my age.'

'And not a bad climber for such a teeny-tiny child,' he admitted. 'You crept up the creeper?'

'If you can, I can,' she boasted.

'Well, don't blame me if you fall and die on the way down,' he said. 'It's harder on the descent.'

'OK, OK,' said Tima, sitting up and pulling down the hood of her black zip-up top. 'We all know you're good at this kind of thing. Freakily good.'

Spin narrowed his eyes. 'Compliments? My. How nice of you. What do you want?'

'I need you to climb up something else,' said Tima.

'Just you? Not "we"? What happened to the rest of the Wide Awake Club? Where's Elena? Matt?'

Tima pulled her phone out of her pocket. The glow from its screen lit up her face. 'Elena is at home; she had a bit of a day today.' She showed him the BBC News website on the screen. The headline on it read:

TEACHER & STUDENTS SWEPT AWAY IN FREAK BORE WAVE

'Elena was *swept away?!*' He felt a pulse in his throat and pushed it down. What did *he* care?

'No—she only got a bit wet,' said Tima. 'The animals warned her. She would have stayed dry if anyone had listened to a word she said. She was yelling at them to get away from the wave but they were too dense to move.'

'The *Wiggenhall Wave* swept people away?' Spin said. 'It's only a metre high! What were they doing—paddling?'

'I don't know all the ins and outs,' said Tima. 'And anyway, it's not Elena I'm worried about right now. I know she's OK. She got some otters to save them, anyway.' She waved her hand as if this was of no consequence; like kids went around asking otters for help every day.

'Fine,' he said, blinking. 'All in a day's work for Supergirl. So what *are* you worried about?'

'Matt,' said Tima.

'Oh,' said Spin.

'He's . . . trapped.'

'In a well?' said Spin. 'Under a steamroller? Inside his own tiny mind?'

'In his flat.'

'Oh my.' Spin lifted his spiky-nailed fingers in a fan of dismay. 'Car-wash Boy's been grounded? How will we all carry on?'

'Stop being so sarky,' said Tima. 'Grow up.'

Spin said nothing. He retracted his black claws and stared at her stonily. When she said nothing further he just shrugged. 'You're right. I should go home and rethink my life.' He was about to trigger more smoke and vanish when she surprised him by grabbing his hand.

'Spin! I need your help. Matt was in court today . . . he nearly got sent to prison for stealing a car.'

'*Did* he?' Spin chortled. 'Little tinker!'

'He *had* to steal it. It was a matter of life and death,' said Tima. She glanced away for a moment, letting his hand go, and added, softly. '*My* life and death, as it happens.'

'Oh,' said Spin.

'So . . . anyway . . . his dad has put a massive padlock on the flat door and taken the key, so now he can't get out at nights and meet us.'

Spin was unimpressed. 'He has a bedroom *window*, hasn't he?'

'Yes—but it's over a really big drop,' said Tima. 'Onto concrete. But . . . there is the canopy; the car wash canopy nearby. You got up on it that time when we needed to wake Matt up. And . . . I think it might be possible for Matt to get down. I've got an emergency escape ladder, but there's no way he's going to be able to sneak that up into his room right now. His dad's on his case *all the time*.'

'So . . . let me get this right. You're after a ladder delivery and rescue service? From me?'

'Come *on*, Spin.' Tima stood up and looked him squarely in the eye. 'Don't tell me you're not interested. You're *so* bored. You know it. This is just the distraction you were after.'

'Don't presume to know what I'm after, little girl,' said Spin.

'OK. Well, never mind.' She turned and walked away.

Spin watched her go right to the edge of the roof and put one leg over. Then he set off in pursuit. 'Wait,' he called. 'You'll break your stupid neck.'

CHAPTER 4

'. . . cause of the freak waves on the Severn, the Dee, the Mersey, and the Great Ouse is still unconfirmed. Joining me in the studio is Dr Stephen Baxendale, an earth scientist specialising in tidal patterns, based at the University of East Anglia.'

Elena lay awake on her bed, watching the iPlayer repeat of the day's news. The presenter turned to the man on the red couch and asked: 'What can you tell us about the causes of these freak tidal waves, Dr Baxendale? And what do you think happened today?'

The scientist smiled warmly but then drew down his dark grey eyebrows. 'It's certainly a very rare occurrence. We get tidal bores frequently around the UK and today they *were* expected as a result of the spring tide—just not at quite this height. Forecasting isn't perfect of course; nature is never totally predictable. Sometimes we get it wrong.'

'So what might have caused this?' pressed the presenter, frowning under her blonde fringe. 'Climate change?'

'It's possible,' said the scientist, 'but not definite. It's possible there has been a submarine landslide somewhere off the Norwegian coast, which could well have caused a surge in the North Sea. Seismologists are checking their data.'

'But could that really affect us all the way down our east *and* west coasts?' asked the presenter.

'Possibly,' said the expert. 'It's surprising how far the effects of even small changes can be felt. Tides are also influenced by the moon, of course, and we are in a full moon phase. Our experts are checking satellites for any anomalies in the Earth's atmosphere which might also have led to this.'

The presenter's brow got even more furrowed. 'Anomalies? Should we be worried? Happily, this time, nobody was badly hurt . . . but what about next time?'

'The thing about freak weather phenomena is that they *are freak*. They happen very rarely,' said the scientist, 'so there's really no need for panic. We'll find out what happened and let the media know—and it's almost certain to be something very mundane.'

He smiled again and Elena hit pause. She stared at his face and she said: 'Dr Baxendale, you're lying.'

She could read it, clear as day, in the man's expression. But the presenter had seemed to accept it and swiftly moved on to another item.

She supposed she should be happy that the story wasn't

bigger. Mr Cochrane, Dan Spelman, and Megan Vasili had only *nearly* drowned. They'd all been recovered, clinging together on a wooden pontoon about a mile upriver. They'd been treated for shock and exposure and kept in hospital for the night, under observation for symptoms of secondary drowning. So far there had been no mention in the media of otters coming to the rescue. She guessed that in the turmoil of the raging water, they might not have realized exactly who—or what—had come to their aid. The buzz from kids at school on social media was that some local dogs had swum after them and dragged them out.

Although she hadn't seen it herself, she knew it was the otters that *had* saved them. She'd got the update minutes before she and the other students had been shepherded back to the school bus. News had spread back along the waterlogged banks and undergrowth, passed from mammal to mammal and then transmitted to her in fleeting, disconnected images and sensations, the last bit from a rat who edged out from beneath some dripping brambles and stared up at her, its whiskers trembling as it imparted the news until Jessie suddenly squealed: 'Oh my *god*—it's a rat!' and the creature had fled.

Elena's odd telepathy with the animal world would be difficult to describe to anyone who wasn't a Night Speaker.

It would be harder still to explain how it had all begun; with the beam which travelled through her room every night at the same time. It had been going on for nearly a year now—for the first few months at exactly 1.34 a.m. every morning, waking her as reliably as an alarm clock. Waking Matt and Tima too. Between late October and late March it had arrived on the dot of 12.34 a.m., after the clocks had gone back across the winter months. But since the UK had returned to British Summer Time two weeks ago, it was back to its 1.34 a.m. slot.

Speaking of which . . . Elena sat up in bed and checked her clock. The beam would be here in three minutes. She had thought she might try to rest at home tonight, even if sleep wasn't possible—and it never was, for several hours after the beam came through. The freak wave had, well, freaked her out. Freaked *everybody* out. They'd all been delivered back to school, minus the nearly-drowned teacher and students who were being ambulanced to Thornleigh A&E, by late morning. Parents were texted with brief details and students were allowed, if they chose, to go home to recover from the shock.

Elena had stayed at school, getting her history project done in the library, texting to Mum that it was OK—she was *fine*—and she'd be back at the usual time. Mum had got some of the details on the lunchtime news, of course, and phoned immediately after the report. Eating a sandwich in the common room, Elena had picked up straight away. 'Seriously?' Mum said. 'You nearly got swept away by a tidal wave and now you want to stay at school to do a history project? You should be at home, crying and stuffing chocolate like a proper teenage girl!'

'I'm just . . . normalizing,' Elena had said, laughing. Which was true. Back home at teatime, she'd played the whole thing down. Someone had, of course, filmed the whole thing on a mobile phone, though, catching the grey wave rearing up across the bridge; the blurry yellow outline of Mr Cochrane and the others slaloming across the wall and into the river.

'It looks worse than it was,' she'd said, into her cup of tea.

Mum had narrowed her eyes. 'Oh right. Of course. Nothing to worry about at all.'

But the network BBC news had caught the fuller story by the 10 p.m. bulletin. Who knew that there'd been freak tidal bores all around the country? Mum had gone to bed by then, drowsy with her medication, so Elena hadn't needed to manage her worry. Mum hadn't had a bipolar episode for quite a few months now and Elena really wanted to keep it that way.

She'd gone to bed herself, at ten thirty, and drowsed fitfully before checking the news bulletin again on her phone. That scientist . . . there was something he wasn't saying. Something . . . Maybe she *should* go out and see Tima and Matt tonight. Maybe she should talk it all through with them. If Matt could escape his flat, that was. Elena hadn't heard anything from Tima since her text shortly after midnight, which read:

Operation Get Matt Out underway tonight. ☺ Will let you know how it goes! Take it easy. xxx

Maybe she should text for an update.

But then . . . aaah. The beam. Here came the beam . . . the long, low, golden note of it swelling like a distant choir and a fizzing, bubbling thin stream of light that was almost, but not quite, invisible. As reliable as sunrise and sunset, the beam swept through her room, through her *soul*. It had taken away her quality of sleep but given her an amazing quality of life and she loved it, loved it, *loved* it.

When it was gone, Elena shook herself out of her rapture, let out a long breath and glanced at the digital clock on her bedside table.

It wasn't 1.34 a.m.

It was 1.33.

She blinked and then it was 1.34.

'What the *hell* . . . ?' she murmured. Was something wrong with her clock? It was a satellite clock, like her phone; it *couldn't* go wrong . . . could it?

She stared all around her bedroom, as if the beam might nip back in and explain why it had shown up early. It had *never* been early before. It had never varied by one second. Ever.

Elena felt the knot return to her belly. Something was wrong. Something was definitely wrong. There was no way she was going to get any rest now—and absolutely zero chance of sleep. She might as well give in, get up, and find her friends.

CHAPTER 5

'So . . . are all your vampire tricks in your coat pockets?' Tima sped up a little, her heavy shoulder bag clunking against her hip, to keep her place next to Spin as he loped through the trees. With his black cowl pulled up over his pale hair it was difficult to see him, but he was using a thin pen torch, swinging it to and fro, low across the woodland path to pick out any obstacles. Anyone else would have told her she was insane to go into a wood with someone like Spin. She wasn't totally sure she would disagree with them.

'I'm not a magician,' he snapped, striding on and making barely a sound on the leaves and twigs.

Tima grinned to herself. She'd hit a nerve. Good. He deserved it. The first time she'd encountered Spin he had scared her almost to death, chasing her through the dark; a cackling funnel of smoke. Who knew how it would have ended if Matt and Elena hadn't come to her rescue?

His whole *creature of the night* thing would be laughable ... except he was really, *really* good at it. He could climb and run and virtually *fly* like something supernatural. He had fangs ... sometimes. He used hidden light effects to get a glow across his moon-white face or make his eyes burn red. He could fight like a Marvel character and even vanish in a cloud of smoke. She would love to know how he did it.

OK, so there was a good reason for Spin's vampire identity issues. Last autumn they had discovered that he really *couldn't* stay out in the sun. It wasn't just some pseudo game—it was a real condition. Erithropoietic protoporphyria was an inherited disease which meant daylight—and a lot of other light too—was agonisingly painful for Spin. Tima could sort of understand why he'd gone weird and decided to 'be' a vampire. In reality, although he had once sunk his fangs into Matt's neck, Tima didn't think he'd ever *actually* drunk anyone's blood. She couldn't swear to it, though.

If it weren't for the fact that Spin had—reluctantly—helped them a few times over the past year, when they'd been in some serious, end of the planet level trouble, she would *no way* be hanging out with him.

But after getting the note from Lucky, she knew she had to do something.

Yeah, well . . . about that . . . Matt had written, in hard black pencil that always seemed to look angry on the paper. Dad's just put a massive padlock on the flat door to stop me ever going out again. Don't know what to do. Could get out of the window but the drop will probably break my legs. This might be the end of my nights out for a while. Text all this to Elena for me, yeah? And tell her I'll see her tomorrow at school.

Tima was furious at Matt's dad. He worked his son like a slave in that car wash and then, when Matt needed his support the most, he just put him on some kind of house arrest! Of course, Matt refusing to explain why he'd taken the car probably wasn't helping. He wouldn't tell his parents the truth—and that was understandable—but couldn't he lie? Make something up?

Apparently not. Matt hadn't wanted her advice. He wasn't good at accepting help from anyone. Tima gulped as she ran along in Spin's wake, feeling the squish and the poke of the woodland floor through her soft-soled jazz shoes, a sudden thought occurring to her. How would Matt react when *Spin*, of all people, showed up with a solution to his problem? Matt *hated* Spin.

'Spin . . . slow down,' she hissed.

Spin turned around, instinctively activating a blue light, somewhere in the collar of his silk coat, which uplit his angular features eerily.

'Do you *have* to do that?' Tima put her hands on her hips.

'It's my thing,' said Spin. 'What's your problem? Big bag too heavy for you, little princess?'

Tima glared at him and hoisted the heavy bag higher. It had been feeling heavier and heavier since she'd hauled it quietly out past her front door while Spin lurked behind the hedge. 'I can manage,' she said. 'Although a *nicer* person would probably offer to carry it.'

'When did I ever give the impression of being *nice*?' he asked, arching an eyebrow. The uplighting made his turquoise eyes gleam in a chilling, supernatural way.

Tima sighed. 'Look—I'm just a bit worried about how we do this . . . with Matt and you . . . *you know*?'

'Oh . . . you mean you're concerned that Matt still wants to kill me?' said Spin, breezily.

'No . . . I don't think he still wants to kill you.'

'Shame. I've always enjoyed our little fights,' sighed Spin. 'Especially that time with the wooden stake in the graveyard; that showed real commitment—and an unexpected sense of theatre. What's the score so far? Oh . . . three or four-nil to me, I think.'

'If we're keeping score, *I* once saw you off at gunpoint,' Tima pointed out.

'And *I* saved your life in that underwater mausoleum,' said Spin.

Tima rolled her eyes. 'Look . . . just . . . stop! Be serious. Help me out here.'

Spin smirked and plucked the bag off her shoulder.

'That's not what I meant!' said Tima, trying to grab the bag back. 'I just think maybe I should talk to Matt, before you show up. Let him know what's happening. See if I can call Lucky back to me . . . send another note.'

'Fuss, fuss, bother, and itch,' said Spin. 'Do what you want.

I'm getting this job done *my* way.'

And he turned and sprinted away into the dark, leaving her gaping after him in frustrated fury.

CHAPTER 6

Matt was woken from a deep, dreamless sleep by the beam coming through. He'd gone to bed early to get away from Dad. The atmosphere in the flat over dinner had been grim. Poor Mum had made his favourite meal—cottage pie. It was her way of celebrating that her son hadn't gone to prison.

After they'd eaten it in silence Matt had utterly surprised himself by getting up from the table, walking around to where Mum was gathering the plates to wash up, and giving her a hug. At fifteen he was now taller than her and able to fold her in his arms as if *he* was the parent. 'Thanks, Mum,' he said, while his father gaped across the salt and pepper pots.

Her surprise and then delight was obvious. And then, catching the look on her husband's face, she'd gently pushed away from him and said: 'Well—you're welcome.'

'How about a sorry, then?' said Dad. 'Sorry for what you've put her through?'

Matt didn't answer. He just left the room and went straight to bed. He half expected Dad to come raging in after him and was quite ready to turn around, raise his fists, and take him on.

But Dad didn't follow.

It had been an exhausting day. He'd had to clean three cars before dinner; no matter that he'd just escaped prison. If he *had* gone to prison that day his father's workload would have gone up massively; he'd have had to employ someone to help him—pay out proper money for it. That would have been unbearable for him.

Matt did get a little money for his work. A very little. Well, well below minimum wage. Sometimes none at all when Dad decided he couldn't afford it. Matt was quite tempted to get himself a weekend job at a rival car wash, just to see the look on his father's face.

Sleep had claimed him within minutes of getting into bed and he felt better for the extra hour as the song of the beam lullabied him awake. He glanced at the windowsill, looking for the familiar silhouette of Lucky, but it wasn't there. This didn't worry him. He often urged her to go back to her family of fellow starlings for the night. She was a colony bird and he worried that it wasn't good for her, spending her time roosting alone to be near him. In warmer weather, he left the window open and she could come and go as she pleased. She was lightning fast and shot outside the second anyone knocked on his bedroom door or attempted to open it.

The night was quiet and he could dimly hear his father's snores. Matt went out to the toilet and then padded, barefoot, in just pyjama bottoms, to the front door to examine the padlock. It was immense . . . like something out of a cartoon. It was a **BIG STATEMENT** from his dad. *I am in control of you! You go nowhere without my say so!*

Matt briefly wondered where the key was. Definitely under Dad's mattress. Dad was incredibly old-fashioned like that. Lucky had once stolen a wallet for Matt and he was certain she would happily get the key, if he knew where it was—but even she would struggle to get it out from under the weight of his sleeping father. Matt sighed as he headed back to his room. He had an amazing superpower, but all it took was one padlock and a fat bloke on a mattress and he was stuffed.

It was 1.41 a.m. There was no way he'd sleep again tonight. Sometimes he managed a bit of a doze around 5 a.m. but he could tell that wouldn't happen this time. He was *burning* to get out into the dark and find Elena and Tima. Burning to tell them about the courtroom, about standing up to Dad.

He flopped back onto his bed, exhaling loudly, and then sat bolt upright, sucking air back in again, as four black-taloned fingers appeared over the edge of his windowsill. He leapt to his feet as another four joined the others, gaping as first a gleam of light and then a pale face emerged, grunting quietly.

What the . . . ?! Matt swiped up the cricket bat from under his bed and ran towards the intruder, ready to swing it down and break those fingers.

'Best not,' hissed a low voice. 'If you break one of my nails I will break your face.'

Matt gaped in shock. Hanging below his window was *Spin*. He let the weapon drop slightly, but still held it tightly. 'What the hell are *you* doing here?'

'Be a love and invite me in, will you?' said Spin.

Matt gritted his teeth. 'You're *not* a vampire.'

Spin suddenly bounded up and over the sill like a gymnast, landing silently on the carpet. 'Well, I like to be polite,' he said. Then, tilting his head, he peered at the wooden bat. 'Good to see that's not sharpened like the last one.'

'Get out of my room,' growled Matt. 'I am not in the mood for your stupid party tricks.'

'Well, no, I imagine you're not,' said Spin, in that incredibly irritating, singsong tone he loved to use. 'Nearly ending up in the clink must have taken it out of you.'

'I'll take it out of *you* if you don't get out,' warned Matt, raising the bat higher. Once again he readied himself for a fight—a much tougher fight than he might have faced with Dad. Spin was a black belt in some martial art or other. It stung Matt to remember the number of times Spin had defeated him.

But, once again, no fight came. Spin just turned back to the window and pulled on a thin rope which was attached to his belt. With some muffled thuds, a large, bulky grey bag emerged at the sill. In spite of himself, Matt leaned across and peered over Spin's shoulder as the boy lifted the bag into the room. What the hell . . . ?

Spin pulled something bright and gleaming out of the

bag. It seemed to be a roll of metal batons, attached to thick red, corded rope. 'A little gift from Tima,' said Spin, without glancing back at him. 'She would have delivered it herself but she can't climb as high as I can. Or . . . as quietly.' He cocked his pale head. 'Listen . . .'

Matt realized there was some heavy breathing—and some quite unladylike cursing—below the window. Pushing past Spin he peered over the window ledge and saw Tima dragging a crate towards the foot of the wall, four or five metres below. She was wearing her usual cat burglar get up, all in black, with her long dark hair in a high ponytail.

'What is going *on*?' he hissed down at her.

She looked up at him and grinned, awkwardly. 'I found a way for you to get out,' she whispered back. 'But I had to get Spin to bring it. Sorry—I can't climb like he can.'

Matt turned, dazed, to see that Spin was clamping one end of the rope and metal batons to the window sill with two C-shaped, rubber-tipped metal brackets.

'It's an emergency escape ladder,' Spin said. 'You attach it like this . . .' He showed Matt how the mechanism worked, simply hooking across the sill and counterbalancing. 'Your weight holds it in place,' he said. 'Just climb over carefully and it'll hold firm. You'll need some decent upper body strength to use the rope ladder bit without swinging about like a brain-dead monkey. I'm not sure about your brain but I guess all the car washing has made you pretty fit.'

Matt put down the cricket bat and stared as his old foe let the rope ladder part fall quietly down from the sill.

'Don't go all soppy on me,' said Spin, straightening up and raising an eyebrow at him. '*I* didn't get it for you; she did.'

The clamped end tightened against the sill, there was more muted grunting and suddenly Tima's face appeared, beaming. 'It *works!*' she said.

Matt hauled her through the window until she stood, wiping some brick dust off her stretchy black jeans. 'Where did you get it?' he asked.

'Home,' she said. 'Dad had a big worry about house fires and got this for my room last year. It's been sitting in my wardrobe in case of emergency. And, well, I think this *is* an emergency. And I don't need it at home; I could easily climb down from my window without it. I have done, before now.'

Matt felt speechless. He sat back on his bed, trying not to look at Spin who was wandering around his room, picking up his stuff with languid curiosity.

'Well?' said Tima. 'Aren't you going to try it?'

'Yeah, of course,' murmured Matt. 'But . . . once it's down, it'll be visible, won't it? If anyone looks up; a dead giveaway.'

'There's a cord on it,' said Tima. 'You pull it up again, like a blind, and leave just the cord dangling down. And the cord's red, so it won't show against the red brick. Try it!'

Matt shook his head and felt a slightly hysterical laugh tickling his throat. He was . . . *touched* . . . that was the word. That Tima would go to so much trouble for him was . . .

'Come *on!*' She literally jumped up and down as if she was five, not eleven.

Matt grinned, shook his head, and pulled his trainers out

from under the bed. 'You two go first and I'll get dressed and follow you.'

CHAPTER 7

Elena reached the hide before anyone else. She'd texted Tima
that she was coming out tonight after all and to meet her at
the Night Speakers' retreat deep in the woods. The hide had
been put up years ago, high in a cluster of trees, by the Forestry
Commission. A metal ladder led up to it but you'd have to be
looking for it to spot it, overgrown as it was with ivy. They had
all taken care to leave the ivy as intact as possible whenever they
climbed up or down; it was the best disguise.

She was about to put her foot onto the lower rung, shining
her thin pen torch beam into the undergrowth, when she sensed
movement and saw a few flickers of light; the others were
coming. Tima must have got Matt out of his locked-up flat.
Elena grinned and hissed: 'You escaped!'

Tima stepped around an oak tree, grinning back. 'You can't

keep a Night Speaker caged for long,' she said.

'We've set up an escape ladder,' said Matt. 'You climb down and then pull on this cord and the whole lot shoots back up again, out of sight.'

'That's brilliant!' marvelled Elena. 'Tima, how did you get it to him?'

'Well . . .' said Tima. 'I had some help.'

Elena felt a coolness in the air and then there was a snap of blue light and a familiar face burst into view, uplit, horror film style, smiling lazily. 'Yoo-hoo,' said Spin.

Elena gulped. 'Well,' she said, not quite knowing how to arrange her face. 'I didn't think we'd see *you* again.'

There was a moment of silence in which Spin probably came as close as he ever would to looking awkward.

'I found him,' said Tima. 'Or rather my midges found him.'

Elena glanced at Tima with a flash of disapproval; they had all agreed not to seek Spin out again after their last encounter. It had all been too . . . costly.

'Look, we *needed* him,' protested Tima. 'Who else could climb up to Matt's window? It's not like I could ring the doorbell and deliver an emergency escape ladder to him, is it?'

'Fair enough,' said Elena. She glanced back at Spin. 'It's good to see you,' she said, quietly.

'Have you got some cocoa?' asked Tima. 'Oh *please* tell me you brought cocoa!'

'I did,' said Elena. 'Of course I did. Let's get inside and have some.'

They made for the ladder but Spin held back. Matt rolled

his eyes. 'Seriously?' he snapped. 'The vampire invitation thing again?!'

'I was just wandering down memory lane,' sighed Spin. 'Remembering our last encounter in your little Famous Five treehouse den.'

Matt squared up to him immediately. 'If you ever put your stupid fake fangs anywhere near me again—'

'Oh for god's sake, just invite him in!' shouted Elena, halfway up the ladder.

But when she looked back down Spin was already gone.

Matt shrugged up at her. 'I *was* going to,' he said. 'I mean . . . he helped. I still think he's a grade A tw—'

'Attacking him with a wooden stake that time didn't help,' said Tima. 'I mean . . . it just encourages him.' She giggled. 'Come on,' she said. 'I want to hear all about your court thing . . . and Elena's tidal wave thing.'

'Tidal wave?' Matt blinked and then followed Tima up the ladder.

'There's something funny going on,' said Elena once they were all settled with mugs of hot chocolate, their faces lit up in the golden glow of the little paraffin heater they'd brought up the ladder.

The hide was pretty comfortable these days. They'd fixed the hole in the roof, put thick plastic across the long low window, insulated the walls, and even made a proper trapdoor with a lock, which they could close and secure when they all left the hide before dawn. If someone *did* spot their leafy den, they'd struggle to get into it. Each of them carried a key to the padlock with them at all times.

'There's always something funny going on,' said Tima. 'We're Night Speakers.'

Elena shook her head. 'This is something . . . different. Did you notice what time the beam came through tonight?'

Matt shrugged. 'No. I wasn't checking. It's always the same time—1.34. Well, apart from the winter months when it was 12.34.'

'Did you notice the time?' Elena asked Tima.

Tima frowned, thinking. 'No. I was already awake, worrying about how to get the rope ladder out of the house. I felt it come through, of course, but I didn't look at the time.'

Elena took a breath. 'Look . . . I may be wrong. I mean, my clock might be wrong. But when the beam came through tonight . . . it was early.'

There was a moment of disbelief and then confusion. 'How early?' asked Matt.

'I'm not sure. It might only have been a second. I just looked and saw one thirty-three. Then a second later it was one thirty-four.'

They were all silent for a moment.

'Your clock was slow,' said Matt.

'It's satellite-linked, like my phone,' said Elena. 'It can't be slow.'

'A glitch . . . ?' said Tima with a wan smile. 'I mean . . . even intergalactic inter-dimensional beams can have an off night.'

Elena nodded. 'Yeah . . . I guess. It doesn't necessarily mean anything. It's just . . . the wave too. Being much bigger than everyone expected. Two weird things in a matter of hours. Not big weird things . . . but . . . two of them.'

She told them everything that had happened that morning, ending in the latest news reports she'd picked up before deciding to head out to meet them. 'So it wasn't just the Wiggenhall Wave,' she said. 'There were freak tidal events all around the coast. Just small ones; nothing catastrophic. But even so. There's something . . . off-kilter.'

'What are the animals saying?' asked Matt. 'Lucky hasn't mentioned anything.'

'Nothing from the insects or spiders, either,' said Tima.

'It's small,' said Elena. 'Something so small that, unless you're right in the way of it, you wouldn't notice.'

'So,' said Tima, raising her mug. 'Maybe . . . just *maybe* . . . it's not our problem . . . ? At least I hope not, because I'm on holiday next week! And I really don't want to have to save the planet while I'm in Dubai.'

Elena forced a smile; Tima had been talking about the Dubai trip for weeks; planning to meet up with her cousin out there and expecting to see all the sights—she was especially looking forward to communicating with scorpions if she got the chance. 'I'm sure it's nothing,' Elena lied. 'Go on, Matt. Tell me about court. How scary was it?'

And as he told them all about it she did her very best to believe her lie. This really *might* not be a problem *they* needed to worry about, for a change.

Only . . . she just knew it was.

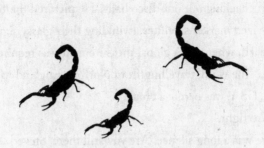

CHAPTER 8

Dr Chase Hamner stared at the monitor for a good five minutes, almost unblinking. His statue-like exterior was in deep contrast to the firestorm going on in his brain ... and quite a few other internal organs.

Around him in the IERS hub other desks were empty and most of the lights were out. There was nobody to ask what was wrong.

Eventually, noting it was 3.12 a.m. on his side of the Atlantic and over in the UK it would be breakfast time, he picked up his phone with a shaking hand and dialled the home number of Dr Stephen Baxendale. The phone was picked up on the second ring.

'Tell me I'm wrong,' said Stephen.

Chase drew a long breath. 'Well ...' he said, still trying to process the words through what felt like a thick fog of shock. 'I've been checking out our disco balls.' He pictured the tiny, football-sized marker satellites, twinkling their glassy signals back to earth whenever a global measurement was required.

'And?' The word, travelling from Norfolk, England to Virginia, USA, was barely a croak.

'You're right.'

There was a long silence. 'Are you still there, Steve?' asked Chase, at length.

'Just about. You?'

'I'm . . . what's a good English word? *Flabbergasted.* Yeah. That's the word. I've checked the lasers, I've checked the telemetry; I've checked everything I can think of. I've been here twelve hours straight and I can't think of anything else to check. So . . . I can only conclude that . . . it's a *fact.* In the past twenty-four hours, Earth has slowed down by a second.'

'A second,' repeated Stephen. 'A full second?'

'Yup.'

'Out of nowhere? Standing start?'

'Pretty much.'

'And . . . is it still slowing?'

Chase took another breath. 'It hasn't stopped politely at just one second. It's still slowing down. If it carries on like this, a week from now we'll have twenty-four hours minus three seconds. And by the end of next week . . . nine seconds. The week after that, twenty-seven and after that . . .' Chase gulped as he mentally hurdled a full minute, ' . . . eighty-one.'

'You're sure?'

Chase took a breath. 'Stevo – I am the big bad boss of the International Earth Rotation and Reference Systems Service. If *I'm* not sure, who the hell is?'

There was a pause and then his old friend said: 'What's causing it?'

'I have NO clue. That's what's bending my brain. There's no El Niño, there's no solar flare, no disturbance in the mantle. Nothing volcanic registering any alarm with the seismologists. Just tickles, you know . . . little things. Lower tides in New Guinea . . . higher ones in the North Atlantic; the Ring of Fire's gone eerily quiet. It's, you know, shruggable today but by tomorrow . . . ? We're not the only ones who are gonna notice this.'

'I know,' said Stephen. 'What are we going to do?'

'Me?' said Chase, taking off his spectacles and rubbing the bridge of his nose. 'I'm thinking about crying.'

CHAPTER 9

Matt's community service began the day after his court appearance. He was told to meet up at 8 a.m. with other offenders in a gravel car park at the foot of Leigh Hill. He left early, glad to get out of the house so he could spend some time walking slowly with Lucky perched on his shoulder.

He was OK about picking up litter. Sometimes he did it anyway, when other people weren't looking. Being in close communication with the animal world made him much less able to look away from all the cack his fellow humans dumped on his friends' homes. He'd been known to stuff rubbish into a carrier bag and shove it into a nearby bin. He thought he might even enjoy doing it in a bigger, more organized way.

'Thanks for being there for me yesterday, Lucky,' he said as they neared the car park.

'Yesterday,' echoed Lucky. It was still amusing to hear her emulating his vocal tones. He and she communicated on lots of levels but her natural starling urge to mimic still came out through her buttercup yellow beak. It often made sense, too.

'I don't know how I would've got on . . . not seeing you for three months,' he went on. 'I don't even know where they would've sent me. Or if there would've been any windows.' He shivered, not for the first time, at the close call. He didn't really blame the magistrate or the police, or the Land Rover owner who'd insisted on pressing charges. They could only work with what they had and all they had was a car thief with no explanation—offering no excuse.

As they reached the meeting point he sent Lucky away to her own kind, guessing that she might check in on him during the morning anyway. She followed her own plans.

There were four other offenders; three boys and one girl. They were all around his age and all quiet as the middle-aged man heading up their Community Service Order group kitted them out with gloves, reflective tabards, extending litter pickers and bin bags which they could hook onto belts around their waists. Another man sat in a flatbed truck, keeping a baleful eye on them all.

'Recyc in the blue bags—that's plastic bottles, cans, paper, and cardboard,' said Dave, the CSO co-ordinator. 'Everything else in the black bags. You find any needles or broken glass, you alert me. Understood?'

They all nodded. 'You can call me Boss,' he said. 'And that's what I am. I don't take any nonsense, any lip, any slacking. If I find you skulking around behind a bush, checking your phones, you'll be on report. Is that clear?'

They mumbled yes.

'Yes, what?'

'Yes, Boss,' they all chorused.

The work wasn't hard. It was a warm spring Saturday morning and the gadget for picking up litter was actually quite fun to use. He would have been working a lot harder at the car wash, and in much worse company. Matt kept his head down and got on with it until he noticed one of the other boys—Kyle, his name was—staring at the sky.

'Something's up,' said Kyle.

'What?' asked Matt, wrestling a particularly stubborn plastic bag out of a thorny spray of gorse.

Kyle just pointed.

Matt looked up and saw a small passenger jet high above, marking a white trail through the cloudless sky. The trail cut across an earlier one. Matt realized there were quite a number of trails and at least three jets circling.

'So . . . the airports get busy,' said Matt, shrugging. 'They stack 'em up.'

'They're not landing,' said Kyle. 'Not at Norwich, not at Stansted. Look.' He pointed south and Matt began to understand. There were jet vapours pencilling lazy circles from one horizon to another and tiny white airborne cigars gleaming in every direction. He counted at least a dozen planes—some obviously small, local turboprops, and others high-flying jets from the continent. All of them . . . just circling.

'What's that about?' Matt murmured.

'Oi—you two!' yelled Dave. 'Back to work.'

'But . . . Boss,' said Kyle. 'There's something going on up there.'

'I don't care *what's* going—oh *yeah* . . .' The Boss stopped abruptly, staring up. By now everyone had joined them, all peering at the sky.

'It's terrorists,' said the girl, her dark eyes wide under her scruffy brown fringe. 'Gotta be.'

Dave surprised them by getting out his phone and rapidly deploying his thumbs across it. 'My mate works in air traffic control at Stansted,' he said. 'He'll have the juice on this.'

Thirty seconds later, as they stood, bin bags dangling from their belts, a text came back and Dave's shaggy grey eyebrows rose. 'Whoa,' he said. 'Good day to be on terra firma. The GPS systems have all gone whack. They're having to bring all the planes in manually. There are flights backing up all over Europe!'

'A cyberattack,' said the girl, dolefully. 'Terrorists. I told you.'

A small dark flight was circling faster than the rest. Matt realized it was Lucky, back again. He moved away from the group, resuming his litter picking on a little slope near a thicket of brambles. Lucky landed on a springy runner of thorns just in front of him. 'What's going on up there, then?' Matt asked, quietly. 'Do you know?'

'No,' said Lucky. Or it might have been 'know' as in knowing something. But all he was picking up from Lucky was confusion . . . and a little unease. He remembered how worried Elena had been last night, obsessing about the Wiggenhall Wave. His skin began to prickle.

'*Really?*' he muttered to himself. 'No. Seriously. *No!*'

'Problem, Wheeler?' The Boss was close behind him.

'Just . . . this is disgusting, isn't it?' improvised Matt, pulling what looked like a baby's nappy out of the brambles.

'If I had my way, fly-tippers would be shot on sight,' responded Dave, mildly.

Matt laughed, although he wasn't entirely sure the man was joking. He went on filling his bags and trying not to focus on that growing sense that everything was going wrong in the world . . . again.

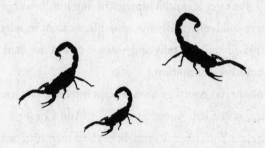

CHAPTER 10

'Well, it's a nice morning to help my daughter go stalking.'
Callie winked at Elena as she pulled into a parking space.

'Mum—I'm not stalking! I just want to . . . meet him. That's all.'

Mum smirked and shook her head as she stopped the engine
and put the handbrake on. She looked well this morning; her
dark blonde hair up in a ponytail and her blue eyes bright. Elena
knew they were alike in looks . . . she just hoped they wouldn't
turn out to be alike in mental health. After years of caring for
Mum whenever she was in a bipolar upswing or downdrop,
Elena's biggest dread was that one day she would start to show
the same symptoms.

But in good times, Mum was brilliant—clever, funny, and
creative—and Elena wouldn't mind a bit of that. She guessed she

took more after her departed dad who was a lot more ordinary.

'I still don't get it,' said Mum, gathering her handbag. 'How come you're suddenly madly interested in a career in science? You see this guy talk on telly and—*pow*—out of nowhere, you've found a brand new ambition.'

'It's not brand new. I've always been interested in science and nature,' said Elena, mostly truthfully. 'And I've seen this guy talk before, on YouTube.' A semi-lie—she'd seen him talk on YouTube between 5 a.m. and 6.15 a.m. *this morning*, before she'd finally dozed off for a couple of hours. He was a good talker, though, and interesting—all about tides and marine biology and earth science and climate change issues. He knew his stuff.

Elena had phoned the University of East Anglia at 9 a.m., expecting to get voicemail and planning to leave a message asking if she could be put in touch with Dr Baxendale. She was surprised when someone in reception picked up—and even more surprised to learn that there was an open day happening at that very moment. 'Normally Dr Baxendale wouldn't be here,' said the friendly receptionist, 'but he's in this morning to do a talk at the open day. Are you interested in being a student here? You could come along.'

'I—yes—yes I am,' Elena had said, before taking notes on exactly where he would be and when. Only afterwards had she realized that there was no way she could get there in time without a lift. So she had asked Mum. And Mum had said yes.

Now, as they got out of the car, Mum was giving her a sharp, assessing look. 'So . . . all of a sudden you're a fan of a fifty-something science professor,' she said.

Elena bit her lip. She'd spent years trying to keep the scary stuff away from Mum; it was just instinctive to bluff it out. Not lying, exactly . . .

'You're not fooling me, Ellie,' Mum said. 'You're on a mission, aren't you? This is something to do with the tidal wave, isn't it? Or maybe it's connected to your strange friends who always look as sleep-deprived as you do.'

Elena gulped. Mum was sometimes worryingly correct with her guesses. 'Yes. You're right,' she admitted. 'I spoke to Matt and Tima about the wave. We all think it's really weird that it was happening all around the country. We think something . . . interesting . . . is going on. And this guy, Baxendale, he knows something but he's not saying.'

'And you think he'll tell *you*?' asked Mum as they reached reception and were handed a University of East Anglia goody bag filled with leaflets and pens. 'He said *nothing* to a BBC news presenter, but he'll tell *you*?'

Elena shrugged and smiled. 'I can be persuasive,' she said.

'I know you can,' Mum said. 'You're clever as a fox.'

Elena blinked, wondering if Mum had seen her chatting to Velma, her vixen friend, in the back garden just last night.

They sidled quietly into the talk, which was more than halfway through and about jellyfish migrating into the seas around the UK. The small lecture theatre was two thirds full, mostly with prospective students and their accompanying parents. Dr Baxendale was a commanding speaker who delivered his lecture with much humour and Elena was quite drawn in. Mum was also absorbed, although she still, occasionally, shot her daughter an appraising glance.

At the end of the talk it was Q&A time. A few hands went up and Dr Baxendale was asked about the degree course he ran, his thoughts on climate change, his favourite jellyfish . . . all the usual stuff. Elena's hand twitched in her lap—two or three times she was on the point of putting it up.

Eventually, just as it looked like the whole thing was wrapping up, Mum grabbed her arm and shoved it in the air. 'ONE OVER HERE!' she sang out and the scientist immediately turned their way and smiled warmly at them.

'What's your question?' he asked.

Elena gulped, shaking Mum off, and then said: 'What do you know about the Wiggenhall Wave?'

They were only four rows from the front; close enough for Elena to scrutinize his micro-reaction while other people in the audience turned to look at her. He blinked and his smile faltered for a fraction of a second, before he said: 'It's a fascinating natural phenomenon. I could talk about tidal bores for hours . . . but suspect I would become a tidal bore myself. I wonder . . . could you hang on so we can have a quick chinwag about it afterwards? I'm pretty much out of time here.'

Elena nodded, trembling slightly—speaking out in public always made her nervous.

'Result!' hissed Mum, nudging her and winking. 'You get to chat him up one-to-one!'

Elena narrowed her eyes at her mother. 'Behave!' she hissed back.

As the last few attendees shuffled out, Elena left Mum in

her seat, with strict instructions to stay put, and then walked up to the front, where Dr Baxendale was gathering some notes on the lectern and sliding them into a battered brown satchel.

'So,' he said, buckling up the satchel. 'What do you want to know?'

Elena waited in silence until he straightened up and faced her. He looked tired, up close; shadows under his brown eyes.

'I want to know what you weren't saying on the BBC yesterday,' she said.

His brow furrowed and he raked a hand through tufty dark grey hair. 'What makes you think I was hiding something?'

'I don't think it,' said Elena. 'I know it.'

He picked up his satchel and let out a long sigh. 'Everyone thinks there's a conspiracy,' he said, trying for jokey but failing.

'I was there yesterday,' said Elena. This stopped him fiddling with his shoulder strap. He glanced at her sharply. 'The bore was three times the height it should have been. That meant the tide was higher than it should have been. Something's going wrong.'

'What's your name?' he asked.

'Elena Hickson.'

'You look a little young to be a student here,' he observed.

'I'm old enough to know there's something wrong,' she said. 'And . . . I get that you wouldn't want to tell everyone and cause panic; that would be stupid. I don't blame you for lying.'

'I wasn't lying,' he said, looking hurt.

'Fudging, then,' she amended. 'I would probably do the same if it was something big and scary. Mass panic isn't going to help anyone.'

'And suppose there *was* something big and scary,' he said. 'Why would I tell *you*?'

Elena smiled. 'Because I might be able to help.'

He looked at her for a long time.

'She's a bit different, this one,' said a voice just behind her. Mum had come over after all. 'If she says she can help . . . she probably can.'

He looked searchingly at Callie now, and he seemed to be on the point of saying something, and then he shook his head. 'I'm sorry—anything I know or don't know is subject to strict confidentiality clauses. Please don't worry about it. Everything's fine.'

And he walked briskly out of the lecture theatre. Elena stood gaping and then Mum grabbed her arm and dragged her along behind him.

'You're going to need to do something,' she said.

'Like what?' squawked Elena, as they hurried down the corridor after the departing scientist.

'Something impressive,' said Mum, as they followed him out of the glass-fronted reception and around the side of the building. 'The sort of thing you do with Velma.'

Elena gaped at her mother. *She knew about Velma?*

'And do it quick,' Mum added, as Dr Baxendale clicked his car key fob, and a Volvo estate parked under a cedar tree chirruped in response. 'He's *getting away!*'

Elena put this astonishing development with her mother into a mental box marked *LATER* and ran after the scientist. He was doing his best to ignore his pursuers as he stashed his satchel on the passenger seat and got in behind the wheel. When the first squirrel landed on the windscreen he looked up in shock at the thud and, mouth dropping open, watched the creature slowly slide down towards the wipers.

The second one landed with another thud on the green bonnet of the car and the third on the roof. Elena walked across to stand beside the open driver door and held out her left arm, making a bridge from the roof of the car to her shoulder. The squirrels ran along her arm and settled, one on her right shoulder and two on her left.

'Are these your . . . your *pets?*' asked Dr Baxendale, staring at the squirrels in amazement.

'Never met them before today,' said Elena, with a shrug. 'But me and the animal world . . . we have an understanding.'

'O . . . K,' murmured the scientist, blinking.

'Go on,' she said, and the squirrels leapt back onto the car and then sat down on the bonnet in full view of the stunned man staring through the windscreen.

'Tell him goodbye,' she added.

All three squirrels turned to look at him, flicked their tails three times, in unison, and then turned and threw themselves back up into the branches of the cedar.

'I do dogs, too,' Elena went on, spotting a man walking nearby with some kind of husky which was pulling strenuously against its harness. 'Watch.' She turned towards the dog, which immediately froze on the end of its lead and swung its head towards her. 'Sing me a song?' she asked, quietly. The husky considered for a moment, its pale blue eyes fixed upon hers while its owner tried to get it to move on. Then it planted its rear end on the grass, lifted its snout and gave a long, carolling howl.

Elena grinned. 'Thank you,' she said, 'better go on now.'

The dog stopped instantly, got up, tail wagging mightily, and went on its way.

'You see,' said Mum, now standing behind her again. 'She's different. You need to tell her what's going on. She really might be able to help.'

He looked defeated. He shook his head, rubbed his tired eyes, and said: 'You'd better get in. We can talk with the doors shut and the windows closed.'

They got in; Elena in the front and Callie in the back.

'So,' said Elena. 'What's happening?'

Dr Baxendale let out a long sigh, his hands resting on the steering wheel. 'The Earth,' he said, 'is slowing down.'

Elena and Callie exchanged glances and then Elena nodded. 'OK . . . by how much?'

'As of last night, by one second,' he said.

'That's not much,' said Elena.

'It doesn't sound like much,' agreed Dr Baxendale. He glanced up through the sunroof. 'But one second's delay is responsible for *that*.'

They followed his gaze and for the first time Elena noticed the planes, circling. There must be at least seven that she could see through the sunroof and the windscreen.

'That'll be the GPS,' sighed the scientist. 'A slowdown of one second is enough to throw out all the global positioning satellites and mess up the air traffic control systems.'

Elena was horror-struck. 'Can't they land?!'

'Yes, they are landing—but it's going to be pretty slow. Nobody in air traffic control is going to be trusting their instruments right now. They'll be bringing them down manually. I expect it's hit the news by now.' He reached for the car radio and then seemed to think better of it and let his fingers drop. 'And of course, it's messed with the tides too.'

'Just *one* second?' murmured Callie.

'It's the abruptness of it,' he explained. 'Imagine I was slowly driving you along and you were drinking a cup of tea. I'd only have to touch the brakes for half a second to make you spill it all down your front. Whatever started slowing down the planet last night came right out of nowhere. Very sudden.'

'But . . . aren't we slowing down anyway?' asked Callie. 'I mean . . . we have to adjust a bit every year, don't we? By a fraction of a second.'

'Yes,' he said. 'Earth has been slowing down for millennia. It slows by about 1.4 milliseconds every hundred years. When the planet formed it was spinning like a top — we had sixteen hour days — so we've slowed down a lot. Slowing down by a second was always going to happen; just not for a very, very long time. Last night the schedule skipped ahead by a millennium or two.'

'So . . . will it settle down now?' asked Elena, taking a long slow breath to calm the sudden fast beating of her pulse.

He shrugged. 'I seriously hope so . . . but according to my friend in the International Earth Rotation Service, this slow down has only just got going. We have tiny satellites out in geostationary orbit; they're about the size of footballs and covered in twinkling glass, like disco balls. We use them as markers for measuring the Earth's rotation. They've just twinkled back some pretty scary numbers. In about six days from now we will have slowed down by three seconds.'

Elena gulped. 'And then . . . ?'

'Well . . . assuming that this phenomenon doesn't stop as suddenly as it started, the next week it'll be nine seconds, the week after that, twenty-seven . . . and the week after that . . .' he took a breath, '. . . a minute and twenty-one seconds.'

There was silence in the car as they took this in. If just one second's delay could cause that tidal wave on the river, thought Elena, what could eighty-one seconds delay do? She shivered.

'So,' said Dr Baxendale, his voice bright and a little shrill, 'you seem to have some rather unusual abilities. Reckon you can stop the end of the world as we know it?'

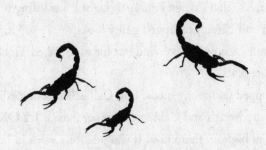

CHAPTER 11

'Well . . . it's a lot warmer here than in the hide,' said Tima, trying to smile as if she wasn't completely freaked out.

Opposite her, on the sofa, Matt was also in a state of shock. 'She knows?' he asked. 'She actually . . . *knows?*'

'I *can hear you*, you know, Matt,' came a voice from the kitchen. Callie came into the sitting room, holding a tray with cake and tea on it.

Elena shrugged and looked a little embarrassed. 'Turns out she's known for ages. I thought I was brilliant at keeping our secret but I . . . underestimated my mum.'

'Don't beat yourself up about it,' said Callie, cheerfully. 'For a long time I thought I was just having delusions. I'd hear you talking in the garden, sweetheart, and when I looked out of the window you'd be chatting with a fox . . . or a bat . . . or, one memorable time just before Christmas, with Matt and a pair of golden eagles. That's when I *really* thought I was losing it.'

Matt and Elena exchanged guilty looks.

'So, um . . . how did you find out for sure?' asked Tima, sipping her tea.

'I stopped taking my meds,' said Callie. Elena immediately took a sharp breath and Callie held up her hands. 'It's OK, it's OK . . . I'm back on them now. It was just for a week in January, so I could stay awake and . . . spy on you a little bit.'

'What did you find out?' grunted Matt, feeding Lucky a cake crumb as she perched on his shoulder.

'That my daughter was leaving the house every night to meet you two . . . sometimes in the company of a fox. To be honest, I was quite relieved. I did think for a while that she might have been seeing that vampire boy.'

'*Mum!*' Elena winced.

'Well, you can't blame me. He did turn up here that time, sweet-talking me for your phone number.'

'That was just so we could save the world from being overrun by killer alien plants,' said Tima.

Callie blinked and then said: 'OK. So . . . Spin, isn't it? Is he part of your group too?'

'No!' said Matt, instantly, while Elena and Tima murmured 'Kind of,' and ' . . . ish.'

'He helps out sometimes,' said Tima. 'When he's not messing with our minds. He's a bit . . . *tortured antihero.*'

'Oooh—like Magneto in X-Men?' asked Callie, looking intrigued.

'He's a bit more Batman than Magneto,' said Tima. 'But . . . not so heroic. He bites.'

'Anyway,' said Elena, rolling her eyes. 'As you can see, Mum knows . . . not everything, because I haven't had time to tell her all of it yet. And I still don't have time because there's something *we* have to tell *you*.'

Tima felt a prickle of fear. Elena wasn't looking at her—or Matt—directly. She hadn't been since they arrived, baffled, at her front door. The text she'd sent had just read: **You need to come to my place tonight. ASAP. Just knock on the door. It's OK.** Matt had received the same message via Luckymail.

'We went to see this scientist today,' Elena went on, putting her mug of tea on the coffee table, but not before Tima had noticed how much the liquid in it was quivering. 'The one who went on the BBC yesterday to talk about the tidal wave. I knew he was hiding something. So . . . I tracked him down. Mum came with me. We made him tell us the truth.'

Tima swallowed, feeling something inside her quake. She had never seen Elena look quite the way she did now.

'What's the truth?' asked Matt.

'The freak tides, the GPS problems with the planes,' said Elena. 'The beam coming through early . . . it's all connected.'

'Connected with *what?*' asked Tima.

'With the Earth slowing down,' said Elena. 'In the last twenty-four hours the revolution of our planet has slowed down by one second.'

They stared at her, silent, trying to take it in and work out what it meant.

'One second . . . is a lot, apparently,' said Elena. 'It's enough to throw all the global positioning satellites out and cause mayhem with air traffic control . . . enough to make the tides go weird.'

'So . . . we've lost a second,' said Matt. 'How bad is that?'

'If it was just one second, once, it would be OK,' said Elena. 'But, according to Dr Baxendale, it looks like it's *still* slowing down. He thinks it'll be three seconds slower by next week. Nine seconds the week after. And about a month from now it'll be more than a minute slower.'

'How can this be happening?' Tima's brain was in overdrive. This *couldn't* be happening, surely? A cold gust of wind billowed the net curtains at the window, like the stage direction in a horror film script. Chilled, she got up and closed the window as Elena went on.

'I don't know how it's happening. That's what we have to find out,' said Elena. 'Fast . . . before everyone on the planet finds out the truth and the whole world starts freaking out. The scientists are trying to find a way to explain it that will stop the public knowing for a while, but they won't be able to do that for very long. We've got to find out what's causing this.'

'Why *us?*' asked Matt.

'Because something bad is happening out in space,' said Elena. 'And Dr Baxendale asked me if I knew how to stop the end of the world as we know it. I told him I didn't... but I might know someone who could.' She reached into her backpack which was stowed down beside the sofa. 'After all—we're the only people I know with a hotline to an intergalactic marshal.'

She pulled a stick out of the bag. It was black, about the size of a marker pen, with a bright green button at one end.

'You're putting a call out to *Carra?*' breathed Tima, feeling goosebumps wash over her skin.

'Who's Carra?' asked Callie.

'Alien,' said Tima, with a swift hand wave. 'Kidnapped me and planned to kill me after I got her nearly stung to death by my wasps.'

'OK,' said Callie.

'But she was actually here to save mankind,' went on Elena. 'Which she did . . . with a bit of help from me, Matt, and Tima . . . and the animals . . . and Spin.'

'OK,' said Callie. She looked just like a mother trying to understand her teenager's social media habits.

'She left this behind,' went on Elena, 'so we could contact her if we ever needed her.' She lifted the stick and put her thumb lightly on the green button. 'I've come close to using this a couple of times . . . when we had to fight the kidnappers taking red-haired kids to Rimagada . . . when we had to stop the Highlands collapsing . . . but I didn't do it. We always found a way by ourselves.' She let out a long breath. 'But this . . . this is too big for Night Speakers to solve on their own.'

'Night Speakers?' queried Callie.

'It's what we call ourselves,' said Tima, quickly. 'We named ourselves after babies in an ancient legend who got left out in the wild by their parents at night, and, if they didn't end up as a wolf's dinner, got the power to speak to animals. They were called Night Speakers. It's a bit posey but it fits.'

'OK,' said Callie. 'Nice summary, Tima. You're a natural.'

'I do my best,' said Tima. 'You're taking all of this very well.'

Callie shrugged. 'Upside of mental illness . . . you build the capacity to get your head around some pretty weird stuff.'

'You are off the scale cool,' murmured Matt, shaking his head in disbelief.

'Cool,' repeated Lucky, with exactly the same level of awe in her tone.

'But, wait,' said Tima. 'If you call Carra and get her help . . . what about me? I won't be here. We're flying to Dubai tomorrow teatime!'

'Assuming the flights are still running,' said Matt.

'Well, my mum and dad checked and everything was fine,' said Tima. 'The air traffic control people must have adjusted.'

'Maybe you should try to talk them out of going,' said Elena. 'Seriously—you don't want to be halfway around the planet while all this is kicking off.'

Tima felt a wave of panic wash over her. 'Mum and Dad have been planning this for *months*. Mum is so excited about seeing her sister. There is *no way* she's going to be talked out of it. Aaargh! Why couldn't the planet start slowing down a *week* from now?!'

'I'm sorry, Tee,' said Elena. 'We can't wait for you. We have to reach Carra now. Tonight. There's no time to lose.'

'It may be that the flights are suspended again,' said Callie, squeezing Tima's arm. 'So you'll get to be here when this . . . Carra . . . arrives.'

'And if not, it might be, I don't know . . . *useful* . . . to have you in another country. You can tell us what's happening over there,' said Elena, trying to be comforting.

But Tima was wracked with frustration and worry. There was no way she could convince her parents to abandon their holiday. She would have to go.

Elena stood up. 'OK, everyone. Outside, I think,' she said. 'Where we can see the stars.'

They all trooped out to the back garden to stare up at the clear night sky. It was 2.15 a.m. and the stars glowed down from the dark velvet blue just as if nothing world-ending was going on among them.

Elena held up the stick and pressed the green button. Tima didn't know what to expect; she imagined a green laser shooting up out of it, away into the heavens . . . or some big, air-shaking noise. But there was just a click. Only a click.

Elena stared at the stick. The green button had turned red. That was all. When she pressed it again it didn't click. It didn't do anything but glow red.

'Right then,' she said. 'Fingers crossed.'

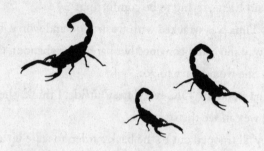

CHAPTER 12

Sundays in Thornleigh were much the same as any small-town Sunday anywhere in the country—lazy starts, sports fixtures, telly, a bit of shopping or DIY, and a chicken roast.

Unless you were Matteus Wheeler and your dad had agreed to valet an entire a fleet of hire cars over a whole weekend, ready for Monday morning customers.

As the world imperceptibly slowed down and an intergalactic marshal might or might *not* be coming to their rescue, Matt knew it was going to be business as usual at Kowski Kar Klean. He really hoped there was *some* chance of sleep first.

He got home around 4 a.m. and pulled on the red cord that dangled down from his window, almost invisible against the red brick. With surprisingly little noise, the rope ladder slithered down to him and he caught the heavy bottom rung in one hand before it had the chance to thwack loudly against the wall. Happily a birch tree grew at the perimeter of the car wash, offering just enough screening at this time of year that any casual passer-by probably wouldn't notice him scrambling up the ladder and over his sill.

Spin was right about his fitness. The constant reach and scrub and drop and scrub and climb and scrub and wax on and wax off of his job meant his core fitness was excellent. If he'd gone to the gym every day instead of working like a slave for his old man, he still might not have gained the six-pack he currently had, or the wiry strength in his legs, arms, and shoulders. Of course, he also might not have gained a weary hatred of soap, wax, filthy car ashtrays, and stinky chemical air fresheners that dangled from rear view mirrors . . . and his dad.

Scoring one small victory over his father gave him quite a buzz as he clambered into his room, pulled the emergency escape ladder off the windowsill and hid it in his wardrobe. He was still aggravated, though, that Tima had called upon *Spin* to bring it here.

He was even more aggravated to find Spin lying on his bed, staring at the ceiling.

His stream of expletives had to be let out in furious whispers.

'Oh cool it, Car-wash Boy,' said Spin, sitting up. 'I just wanted an update on the fate of the planet.'

'So why come *here?*' snarled Matt. 'You normally stalk Elena when you want to talk.'

'I do, don't I?' said Spin. 'And I was thinking of it, but I realized her mother might be . . . bothered by me showing up again.'

Matt exhaled sharply. 'Were you *listening in?!*'

'For a little while,' said Spin. 'But then someone shut the window. I was tempted to knock and join the party but . . . it's not really my thing. I went back to my crypt.'

Matt stood, fuming, unable to think of what to say next other than *get out.* Part of him, though, was intrigued. Spin approaching *him* was completely unheard of. They'd had so many fights. Suddenly Matt was hit by a shocking truth. So shocking he bumped down on the bed next to his unwelcome guest.

'You're . . . you're *scared,*' he said. When Spin only fiddled with the laces on his fine leather boots, Matt turned to look at him. The older boy's face was in shadow.

A small dark figure landed on the sill and echoed: 'Scared.'

'Oh well, that's *ganging up!*' snapped Spin. He got to his feet and paced the small stretch of carpet between the bed and the window before turning to look squarely at Matt. 'Of *course* I'm scared! Aren't *you?*'

Matt gulped and nodded as Lucky flew to his bunched fist. It was the very last thing he'd ever expected Spin to say.

'We have dealt with some impressive enemies,' said Spin. 'The underworld god, the homicidal botanist from another planet, ginger child traffickers . . .'

'Don't forget the alien mining grubs destroying the Scottish Highlands,' added Matt and felt a little, cheap, buzz of pleasure when Spin looked mystified. 'Ah yes—you weren't around for that one.'

'Whatever,' said Spin, with a wave of one black-taloned hand. 'The point is, we've always been able to take the fight to the enemy—because it's all been *here* on Earth. Well, mostly. Now though . . . if what Elena says is true . . .' He perched on the windowsill, gazing out into the night. With the moonlight shafting across his angular face, he looked like a Gothic painting. 'I've been online, doing some research,' he said. 'There's not much out there at the moment. Just a bit of chatter on the nerdier scientific sites. Nothing confirmed. Not yet.'

'Good,' said Matt. 'If it carries on . . . the slowing down . . . people are going to find out and go crazy. I don't want to be around crazy people.'

'So . . . what are you all doing? What's the Night Speaker plan?' said Spin, still staring out of the window.

'We've called Carra,' said Matt. He didn't see the point of lying. Not now.

'Called Carra?' Spin turned back to stare at him. 'Waspy Wendy?! *How?* I thought she'd popped home to her own dimension after we all saved the planet.'

'She left some sort of communication gadget with Elena,' said Matt. 'Elena activated it in the garden tonight. Weren't you watching *that?*'

'Damn!' said Spin. 'I should have lurked a little longer. So . . . did it work?'

Matt shrugged and put Lucky to roost on his bedstead. 'Don't know. The light went from green to red.'

'Well, that's all fine then,' said Spin, sitting on the windowsill. 'We're saved.'

'Have you got a *better* idea?'

Spin sighed and dropped his head. 'So . . . we just wait for help from the heavens. That's it?'

'Unless *you've* got a plan, yeah, that's it.' Matt, suddenly exhausted, dropped onto his pillow.

'Well . . . I suppose it could *work* for me,' mused Spin. 'If the planet slows to a stop and the sun is on the *other* side, I could be quite comfortable. Night forever.'

'We'd all be dead long before that point,' said Matt.

'I suppose we would,' said Spin. 'Well . . . I'd say it's been nice to chat, but it hasn't, really. Better go home and prepare for the breakdown of law and order, the unravelling of civilization, and total anarchy ruling the streets, I suppose.'

'Is that the best you can do?' Matt felt a surge of anger. 'Go off and brood?'

'I can't think of anything more constructive, can you? I mean I suppose if we all face east and run *very hard* on the spot—'

'Teach me to fight.'

'What?' Spin stood up, narrowing his eyes as if he'd misheard.

'You heard me. Teach me. Teach me to fight like you do,' said Matt, not quite believing his own words. 'If it's going to be anarchy out there, I want to be able to look after myself . . . and my mum.'

Spin tilted his head to one side. 'Your mum?' He raised his pale eyebrows and nodded. 'Well . . . fair enough. We all need to look after our mums. All right then. Assuming the crisis isn't over, meet me at the bandstand tomorrow evening. Around nine.

If you can get away. We could wait until the early hours but, well, we don't know how long we've got, do we? Better snap to it.'

'You . . . you'll teach me?' Matt was astounded.

Spin shrugged. 'It'll keep my mind off the end of all things.'

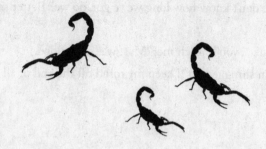

CHAPTER 13

'How much longer do you think we can keep this quiet?'

On the laptop screen, Chase looked bone weary. Stephen wondered if he had slept at all since their discovery. Mind you, nobody at IERS was sleeping right now. It was 8.15 a.m. on Sunday here in the UK and Chase had only left an emergency meeting twenty minutes ago. It was 3.15 a.m. in Virginia.

'A day, maybe? Two?' said Chase, rubbing a hand over his stubbly jaw. 'And that's only if everyone plays ball. Scientists all over the planet are waking up to the anomaly. It'll only take one of them to call up the media.'

Stephen gulped. 'What's the word from the White House?'

Chase shook his head. 'No word. We haven't passed this up the line, yet.'

'You *haven't?*'

'We can't trust this news to *politicians*,' murmured Chase, leaning in to the webcam, so his worried face suddenly loomed closer. 'Not until we have some . . . strategy. The military . . . maybe.'

Stephen nodded. 'I'm supposed to go to Downing Street first thing Monday morning,' he said. 'To brief the Prime Minister.'

'Yeah? When exactly?' asked Chase.

'Breakfast—8.30 a.m.'

'Well, that's just peachy. So we'll *have* to speak to *our* great leader. Same time.' Chase rolled his eyes. 'That means I've got 24 hours to make some kind of plan. A *plan*? I can't even come up with an explanation!'

'Well, about that,' said Stephen.

'Go on!'

'I've been up to Jodrell Bank and spoken to Emma Palliser, my contact there. She was watching our skies three nights ago— and she thinks she spotted something odd around the same time as this slowing anomaly began.'

'Go on!'

'She's still processing the data, but . . . she thinks there was movement in the atmosphere. Something unexplained—for a second, no more—something was picked up in close proximity to the moon. There's no visual, just disturbance readings. She's . . . well she's a bit of a sci-fi fan. Her exact words were "There's something hiding on the dark side."'

Chase stared into the webcam, unblinking. 'You're kidding me.'

'No. That's what she said.'

'Prove it!'

'We're working on that.'

Chase suddenly sat back in his chair. 'Jeeez. What the hell are we going to do? You got any ideas, Stevo? Cause I sure as hell don't.'

'Not really . . .'

Chase was suddenly up close again, narrowing his eyes searchingly.

'What?'

'No, it's nothing.'

'Whatever you've got, I want to hear it.'

Stephen sighed. 'I met this girl and her mother yesterday,' he said. 'They came to an open day at the university. The girl saw me on the BBC. She wanted to know what I was hiding about the unexpected size of the local tidal bores. She was nearly hit by the Wiggenhall Wave.'

'Yeah? And?'

'I . . . I sort of . . . told them.'

'You did *what?*'

'I know, I know . . . but . . .' Stephen sighed and shook his head. 'The girl—she can communicate with animals.' Chase bunched up his face. 'Seriously, Chase—she did it right there, right in front of me. She had squirrels virtually dancing to order—and a dog pretty much singing.'

'You're melting my brain, buddy,' said Chase. 'What's this got to do with anything?'

'Maybe nothing,' said Stephen. 'But . . . she said she knew

someone who could help. Someone . . . from another planet.'

'O . . . kaaaay.'

'Yes. I know. I'm probably losing my mind. But . . .'

'Listen, Stevo—if you think some kind of squirrel whisperer has the answer, you go for it,' said Chase. 'Call her up. See if this alien saviour is on his way because I'm all out of ideas.'

'OK,' said Stephen. 'I'm going to call her. Just . . . keep this between ourselves, all right?'

'You think?! Look—just keep me posted.'

The link went blank and Steve looked at the name and number on his phone. *Elena Hickson.*

He had never really believed he *would* phone her.

CHAPTER 14

Sunday dragged like an injured cat.

Elena and Callie watched the news, drank endless cups of tea, and waited.

In the middle of the kitchen table the black stick glowed red at its tip. And nothing happened.

Tima checked in frequently by text.

Packing now. Up in my room picking outfits for END OF THE WORLD!

What's happening? Any news? :-/

WHERE IS CARRA?

And so on. Elena tried to be calming in her responses:

Will let you know the second I have news!

Nobody's talking about it on telly, radio, or online.

I DON'T KNOW! Just stop worrying. Pack. Have a great holiday. This could stop just as suddenly as it started. And if your flight isn't delayed that's a really good sign.

After a long pause Tima sent back:

Yeah. Btter mk sure I have a gd hol. Might b my last. ☹
xxxx

The call from Dr Baxendale hadn't helped. Elena had confirmed that yes, she had sent the message and no, she hadn't heard back. The disappointment she detected in the scientist's response, as hard as he tried to hide it, made the cold fear in the pit of her belly drop a degree or two lower. One of the country's most respected scientists had called *her*. She had offered to help and given Dr Baxendale her number—but once she and Mum had left the poor man alone in his car, she'd really expected to be politely ignored. How bad were things getting in the real world of grown-up science, that he *had called*?

Elena kept standing over the communication stick, staring at the red light, *willing* it to flash or turn another colour or just . . . do . . . *something*.

In the end, Mum switched off the TV and the laptop live feeds. She dug out a DVD of Disney's *Aladdin* instead and set it playing. She made Elena sing along with all the songs, like a five-year-old. Elena wished she *was* a five-year-old. Where was Carra? What was keeping her? Their alien friend could create corridors from distant galaxies and step through them, from planet to planet, in a matter of seconds . . . at least that's what she'd told them.

Elena had never doubted the truth of this until now.

It was 8.23 p.m. and Tima was now high above Eastern Europe in her business class seat (no delays at the airport according to her texts) when there was a clicking sound at the kitchen window.

'Your friend's here,' said Mum, smiling.

A small bloom of condensation surrounded the tip of a black nose pressed against the glass.

'Velma!' breathed Elena, with both relief and dread. It took something for her vixen buddy to make contact in full view of Elena's mum. She guessed Velma had sniffed out the new normal, here at home, and worked out it was now safe.

Elena opened the kitchen door to find the vixen sitting on the patio.

'Bring her in!' breathed Mum, her eyes wide with wonder.

But Velma got up and walked away, her tail high and her nose determinedly pointing south. At the side alley to the front of the house, the fox paused and looked at them meaningfully.

'I have to follow her,' said Elena, her heart rate picking up and her skin prickling. 'It's important.'

'Of course,' said Mum. 'Can I come too?'

Elena blinked. Involving Mum still seemed so weird. But there was no Tima to call on, and no easy way of contacting Matt unless Lucky dropped by. If Mum wanted to come, she could be useful backup.

'OK . . . I'll just get my backpack,' she said.

'And I'll get mine,' said Mum.

Matt threw Spin on the floor of the bandstand. Spin had *let* him make the throw, of course—it was part of the training—but Matt still experienced a deep thrill to see the pseudo-vampire sprawling at his feet. He wasn't sure quite how *much* the boy was going easy on him. They'd been training for over an hour now and to start with it had been pretty brutal. In fact he'd wondered, at first, whether Spin had only agreed to train him so he could beat him up for larks. But now it did seem to Matt that he was getting better at defending himself. Just as well, since he'd skipped out of his bedroom window at 8.30 p.m. this evening. He'd told Mum he was going to chill out in his own room and would probably go straight to bed later on. She knew he was avoiding Dad so she made no comment . . . there was a chance she might check in on him, though, and find he was gone. He really hoped not.

Spin jumped back up and threw a punch—and Matt blocked it fast. He didn't block the other hand, though, which came up and thumped him in the belly. Then Spin knocked the breath out of him in an entirely different way.

'You're picking up blocking very fast,' he said, as Matt

doubled over and rubbed his solar plexus. 'Must be the muscle memory of all that "wax on—wax off."' He made the circular movements with his hands, smirking. 'Very *Karate Kid*. That was a good block. Not good *enough* for someone like me . . . but probably good enough for your average attacker.'

'It's probably what I need to learn most,' Matt grunted, thinking of his father.

And then Spin took even more of his breath away. 'Your father?'

Matt stared at him, speechless. Had Elena spoken to Spin about his father?

'It won't take much to show him you're not his punchbag any more,' Spin said. 'You're fit and strong and your instincts are good.'

Matt nodded and then Spin kicked him in the chest—but he grabbed the shiny black boot and sent the boy back onto the floor. Then he just stood, still shell-shocked, processing what his long-term foe had just said to him.

'Come *on*, then!' Spin goaded. 'I'm down but I'll be up again in a second if you don't disable me! Knee on chest, grab wrists, pin back . . .'

'Wait,' said Matt, reluctantly stepping away as a small, feathered figure arrived on the balustrade of the old wooden structure. 'I think there's news.'

The starling flew to his bunched left fist and he dropped his head close to hers. A leap of adrenaline made him catch his breath. 'We have to go,' he said. 'Now.'

After nearly forty minutes of scrambling through the dark, across the wooded and brambly slopes on the far side of Leigh Hill, Elena began to wonder whether Velma really knew where she was going.

'Does she actually have a clue where she's leading us?' puffed Mum, scrambling up the latest fold of wilderness, her torch casting a shaky pool of white light across the roots and nettles and eye-flicking twigs in their path.

They were some distance from the part of the woods where the Night Speakers' hide was, in a valley only occasionally visited by walkers or horse riders. Thanks to several massive pylons looming across it, the area was not really high on anyone's beauty spot list. Velma reached a flattened, level area of the hillside, glanced back at them, and then sat down, wrapping her thick red tail around her paws. It looked as if she had arrived.

But at what?

Elena, Matt, and Tima knew that there was some kind of cave around here, somewhere inside the limestone and chalk hill that hung above Thornleigh. They'd already, several months ago, discovered one cave on the northern side where nineteenth-century quarrymen had hacked into the land leaving behind a high inland cliff to hang broodingly over the town. But that cave was not the cave where Carra had come through the corridor.

The beam that woke them every night went to Carra's cave; they knew this. Elena and Matt had worked out its trajectory, through each of their bedrooms and on down through Quarry End Industrial Estate, through the cave which *wasn't* Carra's entry point, and deep into the impenetrable hillside. Matt thought he'd worked out more or less where Carra's cave had to be and he'd spent several nights last autumn trekking around the area, trying to find a hidden opening. He'd gone back in daylight hours too, when he could get away from the car wash—but even with Lucky's help he'd not managed to find it.

Tima had asked her insects and spiders for some intelligence on the hidden cave too—and Elena had asked the mammals. None of them had come back with anything. If there was a corridor cave to the south of Leigh Hill, their animal friends didn't seem to know about it.

Until now, it seemed.

Elena and Callie climbed the slope and reached the flattened place beside the fox just as another thin stream of torchlight swept the area and a small dark creature flitted through it. A *bat?* thought Elena. No. *Lucky!*

'Hey!'

'Matt?' Elena turned to see her friend running up the hillside, followed by something glowing faintly red. '*Spin?!*'

'Yeah . . . he was there when Lucky came to get me,' muttered Matt, looking embarrassed as he glanced back at his shadowy companion.

'Spin . . . was with *you?*' Elena gaped at the pair of them as they reached the flattened spot, somewhat out of breath.

'We had some work to do,' said Spin.

Elena was about to ask *what work* when Velma made a low growling sound—not of warning but of impatience. 'OK—this is where they want us to be,' she said, looking around. 'I've no idea why, though. There's no cave . . . it's just . . . grass and stones.'

They stood in silence for a few moments. Then Spin crouched down, his lightweight black silk coat billowing in the evening breeze. 'What is it, fox?' he asked. Velma gave him a look of contempt.

'Well . . . don't keep us guessing!' Spin went on. 'Or maybe,' he glanced up at Lucky on Matt's shoulder, 'your bunch of feathers could be a bit more forthcoming after dragging us up hills and down dales for the last half hour!'

'Down,' said Lucky, from her roost on Matt's shoulder.

They all shone their torches further down the hillside. It was dark, brambly, and unremarkable.

'Down *where*, Lucky?' asked Matt.

Lucky flew down to his feet, and pecked at some grass. Velma gazed coolly across at the bird but made no move to snatch it. The Night Speakers had learned that animals never preyed on each other in their presence; there seemed to be an unwritten code of conduct.

Spin stood up and tapped his foot on the ground beside the starling. It made little sound, thanks to his soft-soled boots, chosen for ease of running and roof climbing as much as style. 'Hey—clumpy toes,' he said to Matt. 'Come and stamp your leaden feet over here.'

Matt gave him a sour look but he moved across and stamped down hard. A low, dull note rang out. 'It's hollow!' he cried.

Elena dropped to her hands and knees to inspect what had appeared to be nothing more than thin vegetation over packed earth and stone. Velma brushed past her, leaving a hint of fox scent on her cheek, and vanished into the undergrowth further down the hill. She obviously felt her work was done. So . . . what was here?

The boys were still stamping while Callie held her torch steady, bathing the scene in a helpful glow. 'Ssshhh!' said Elena. 'Stop a moment.' She held her head still, her nose tickled by grass. 'I can feel . . . air . . .' She got to her feet, stepped back, and then gave a squeak as she tripped over on her back heel. Her foot had caught on something. Landing with a thud, she immediately scrambled up to see what had tripped her and found a small rectangle of metal rising just above the grass. In the torchlight she read:

1833 LEIGH ARTESIAN WELL

'It's a well!' she gasped. 'We're standing over a well!'

They all dropped and began pounding on the floor, until Callie gave a shout. 'Look—I've found a pull ring!'

The iron ring was mostly sunk into the soil but they dug it out with the screwdriver which Matt was carrying in his backpack. (Elena didn't need to ask why. They'd faced so many dark and terrifying moments over the past year, a weapon of any kind seemed sensible. She had a pretty lethal pair of scissors in hers.)

The ring pulled clear, Matt tugged it hard. No trap door magically opened . . . because it was nailed down. The shape of it was revealed, however, as the wood beneath the thin layer of soil shifted. The screwdriver was put to good use again and inside two minutes the nails lay in the grass.

For a moment they all stood in silence, gathering

themselves. Then Spin leaned over and pulled the circle of iron.
The wooden panel; about the size of half a door, came up with
a hollow crunching noise. It pivoted back and Spin let it drop
away beside the hole.

The hole should have been nothing but blackness.

It wasn't.

A dull, lilac light rose up from somewhere down inside
the shaft, along with an old, wet, musty waft of air. Silhouetted
in the lilac light, they could make out a figure, clinging to an
ancient, spindly ladder.

Elena shone her torch down and exhaled sharply as two
dark eyes glittered up at them, in a tired, white face.

'You took your time,' said Carra.

CHAPTER 15

'Yes, I *was* planning to kill Tima,' said the alien. 'But that was only when I thought she was an Ayotian interloper intent on wiping out all life on Earth. May I have some more cocoa, please?'

Callie wordlessly poured another mug of hot chocolate and handed it over to the tall, dark-haired woman dressed in green leather. Spin was impressed with how quickly Carra had regained her strength and composure. An hour ago, when they'd hauled her out of the narrow well, like a newborn baby, smeared in dirt and blood, she'd been so exhausted she was unable to stand. He and Matt had mostly carried her back to Elena's place. Now she was sitting up straight and her almond shaped eyes were alert and intelligent. Even her shiny dark hair had fallen into shape, neatly plaited to one side of her beautiful face.

'*Mum!*' Elena shook her head. 'Why did you have to ask her about that, of all things?! She's only just got back the strength to talk!'

Callie shrugged. 'Well, sorreee—but Tima did say Carra wanted to kill her last time she was here. I thought it was a good idea to check why . . . just in case she had some fresh reasons to embark on any manslaughter this time around.'

'I was mistaken,' said Carra, through curls of steam. 'Tima, Elena, and Matt . . . even Spin . . . are both human and good.'

'Even *Spin!*' echoed Spin. 'Well, high praise *indeed!* No mention of Tima trying to have you stung to death, I notice.'

'It was a misunderstanding,' said Carra.

Elena sat down opposite Carra and held up both hands to shut the others up. 'First—are you OK? What happened to you down there? Why couldn't you get out?'

'There was a collapse,' said Carra. 'My previous exit was blocked. I had to find another way. It took me . . . several hours.'

'I'm so sorry,' said Elena, looking stricken. 'We were just sitting around watching movies, wondering whether you were going to show up. We had no idea you were already here!'

'But your animal friends heard me and told you to come,' said Carra. 'It is fine. Now. You tell *me*. I think I can guess . . . but why did you call?'

Elena gulped. How to begin?

'The world is slowing down,' said Matt. 'It started on Thursday night—it revolved a full second slower.'

Carra's eyes narrowed. 'And it hasn't stopped slowing, has it?' she said.

'You *know?*' asked Elena.

Carra consulted a glowing watch-like gadget on her left wrist. 'Earth is currently rotating 1.539 seconds slower than it was the last time I was here. The deceleration is at a rate of roughly 0.428 seconds in every twenty-four hours.'

'Why? How?' demanded Elena. 'What are we going to do about it?!'

'Why?' said Carra. 'I'm not sure yet. How? With a galaxy class Ayotian warship parked on the far side of the moon, interfering with the Earth's polar magnetism. What are we going to do?' She took a breath. 'That is not so easy to answer.'

'You mean you can't save us, Waspy Wendy?' asked Spin. 'After all that crawling through a well?'

'Do not call me Waspy Wendy,' said Carra.

Spin bit his lips shut and fanned his fingers in sarcastic apology. To be fair, she *had* been at death's door after hundreds of wasp stings when he'd carried her to hospital last year. That had to be an unpleasant memory. Somewhere inside him, Spin was shaking; scared. His blood disorder meant this was not an unfamiliar situation; when you know that just stepping out of the shadows can almost crush you with pain, you have a healthy level of *scared* just below the surface.

This, though, was a whole new level. Being snippy and annoying was helping him cope.

'Did you know about this before I called you?' asked Elena.

'I was investigating,' said Carra. 'As marshal for the quadrant covering your galaxy, I was aware of some interference in your solar system. I intended to check in but I was busy tracking a criminal on another planet. Once she had been detained I turned my attention to this interference and almost at once I received your call. My sensors and trackers revealed a craft of unknown origin on the dark side of your moon. It was only as I reached the outer edges of your solar system that I was able to identify it as Ayotian.'

'Those Ayotians don't give up, do they?' muttered Elena. She glanced at her mother. 'They were behind the plot to spread alien plants all over the world and suffocate us,' she explained.

'Oh. OK,' said Callie.

'So . . . if that warship is what's slowing the planet down,' said Matt, 'all we have to do is get rid of it and everything goes back to normal . . . ?'

'Absolutely correct,' said Carra.

'So . . . how do we do that?'

Carra closed her eyes for a long moment. Then she said: 'May I have some more cocoa, please?'

Spin noticed Callie's hands shake a little as she poured out yet another mug of cocoa from her battered old saucepan.

After drinking at least half of it, Carra opened her eyes fully and looked around at them all. 'I could call in the support of six or seven Quorat planets in a matter of seconds,' she said. '. . . normally.'

'. . . but?' prodded Spin, as the others just goggled at her.

'As I came through my corridor, it was closing down behind me,' she said. 'The Ayotian ship must have detected me. They are a race with some enviable technology. I had heard they'd found a way to close another traveller's corridor remotely. Until today I did not believe it, but now I see it's true. As long as they are close enough to block my cleftonique signal and close my corridor . . . they have trapped me here on your planet. Perhaps it is because I have arrested one of their own and shamed them— they have made it their business to track my corridors, find my beam frequency, and block it.'

'Wait!' said Spin. 'Are you telling us that this whole slowing down the planet thing is all about *you?* It's . . . personal?'

She tilted her head, pursed her lips, and considered for a few seconds. 'It could be. Or they may just be planning to invade . . . again.'

'Carra . . . what are we going to do?' asked Elena. 'This is urgent. The more the planet slows down, the bigger the tides are. That means,' she gulped, '. . . tidal waves . . . tsunamis . . . earthquakes . . . the magnetic poles going crazy.'

'Yes, it will soon be an extinction level situation,' agreed Carra. 'I must help you . . . but . . .'

'But WHAT?' exploded Callie. 'Get to the bloody point, woman!'

'Well,' said Carra. 'The obvious solution is to trigger a solar flare and destroy the Ayotian vessel.'

'That sounds good,' said Spin. 'It's nice when the sun is *helpful.*'

'But in losing the corridor I have also lost my communications,' Carra went on. 'I need the Quorat to advise me of the precise location of the Ayotian vessel . . . and I cannot reach the Quorat if I have no corridor.' Carra put down her empty mug with a clunk. 'I'm sorry.'

'Can you fix it?' asked Elena in a high, thin voice. 'Your corridor, I mean?'

'No,' said Carra. 'I will need a new one. There are other frequencies I can use to signal to my people . . . but they are too weak here on Earth. I would need to be improbably high in your atmosphere to send the signal.'

'So . . . we climb a mountain!' said Matt. 'We'll take you to Ben Nevis! It's only seven or eight hours' drive from here. We could be there by morning.'

'Mountains are not suitable,' said Carra. 'Too cold and too wet. Too vulnerable to atmospheric pressure shifts. The height need not be so great—maybe a kilometre; high enough to be unpolluted by ground level interference. But warm and dry.'

'Hot air balloon?' suggested Spin.

'The point of projection must be stationary,' said Carra. 'This is why I cannot give you a clear solution. I do not know if it is possible.'

There was a heavy silence around the table as everyone took this in. Spin realized he had really, for a while, believed that his old alien adversary was going to make everything better.

Apparently not.

PING . . .

Elena blinked and pulled her phone out of her pocket. 'Tima,' she said. 'She's just landed in Dubai. She wants to know what's happening.' She slumped, dropping her forehead into her palm. 'What am I going to tell her?'

Spin felt something like a bullet shoot through his brain. A hot bullet of *hope*.

'Tell her she's in **EXACTLY** the right place!' he said.

'Well, *maybe*,' said Elena, rolling her eyes. 'You might as well be having fun to the end.'

'Eight hundred and twenty-eight metres,' said Spin, turning to peer at Carra. 'Would that be high enough?'

Carra frowned, consulted her wrist gadget and then lifted her head. 'Possibly, but . . .'

'Hot and dry and stationary,' went on Spin. 'And eight hundred and twenty-eight metres high.'

He stared at them all as they gawped back at him like idiots. 'Oh for crying out loud! How dense can you be? Tima's right there already. It's in *DUBAI, obviously!* The tower! The Burj Khalifa!'

'Oh my god, yes!' squeaked Callie. 'Tallest tower in the world! It was in that movie . . .'

'What is this?' asked Carra.

'It's the tallest manmade structure on the planet,' said Callie. 'It's like a massive needle of glass and concrete and steel, on the edge of the Arabian Desert.'

'Then we must go there,' said Carra, standing up and grabbing her mud-encrusted kit bag.

'Whoa—hang on,' said Elena. 'It's a long, long way. It took Tima seven hours to get there by plane.'

'Then we must take the plane,' said Carra.

'Have you got a passport?' asked Callie.

Carra nodded.

'I mean . . . an Earth passport, you know? Not an intergalactic one.'

Carra gave Callie a pitying look. 'I would not attempt to travel your planet without the appropriate documents,' she said, pulling a metal case out of the bag and flipping it open to reveal a selection of very authentic-looking passports.

'OK,' said Elena. She looked at her mother. 'Can we afford the air fare?'

'We can bend the credit card,' said Callie, already grabbing their elderly laptop and searching for flights.

Spin watched them thrumming with sudden, excited purpose and felt a little glow of satisfaction. He would never have guessed that this, of all the myriad small facts his eidetic memory stored away, would turn out to be so useful. Then he noticed Matt's expression and felt a sudden, odd kinship with Car-wash Boy.

'Have you got a passport?' he asked, raising an eyebrow.

'Yes,' said Matt.

'So . . . are you going too?'

'I can't afford a flight to Dubai,' said Matt.

Elena glanced at her mother. 'We can pay for Matt too, can't we?'

But Callie was biting her lip. 'I think we're going to max out the card just paying for you, me, and Carra, sweetheart.'

'It's fine,' said Matt with a face that very clearly said *It's not fine.*

Spin felt a creepy, prickly sensation go through him, as if he might be about to vomit. He struggled to hold it down but in the end he couldn't. The whole sentence chucked up out of his throat before he could stop it. 'It's all right, Squeegee Boy. I'll buy you a ticket.'

Matt gaped at him.

'We can't let this be a female-only planet saving,' he added. 'I've got plenty in my savings account. Slide the laptop over to me and I'll buy his,' he said to Elena.

'You mean you carry a bank card around in that Hammer Horror coat?' she spluttered.

'No . . . I carry all my bank card numbers in *my Hammer Horror head*,' he corrected.

Matt looked as if he was in a dream. 'Are we . . . are we all actually going to fly to Dubai?'

'As long as we make it to Stansted by 5 a.m., yes,' said Callie.

'Will you come too, Spin?' asked Elena.

He looked into her blue eyes and suddenly realized how much he'd missed her these past few months. He imagined sharing a flight with her; messing around with the movies and the snacks; watching the clouds below them like an Arctic sea; winding her up about the dangers of air travel . . .

'No,' he said. He glanced at the lamp in the corner. It was the only light in the room and he was as far from it as he could get, but even so it was making his face and the backs of his hands prickle. 'If the light on the plane didn't kill me, the Arabian sun would.'

'You could . . . carry a black umbrella . . .' suggested Elena in a voice that suggested she knew how pathetic that sounded.

'Light bounces,' said Spin. 'I'd need to be in a giant blacked-out hamster ball.'

There was a moment when they all looked at him and Callie

murmured: 'That's really tough, love. It must be hell.'

Spin found he couldn't speak. He took a deep breath and then muttered: 'Better sneak home and get your passport, Matt.'

CHAPTER 16

'Your father went out.' Mum was in the hallway in her bathrobe as Matt sidled out from his room, just before midnight. 'It's his friend's birthday. I told him to go and celebrate. I said I had a headache and I didn't want to go.'

Matt stood still. His mum looked tired, leaning against the doorway to the kitchen. 'Mum . . . I . . .'

'Your life here . . .' She sighed, and looked somewhere over his left shoulder. 'It's not good. You are worked too hard. And your father . . . he is too rough with you.'

None of this was news to Matt, but it was the first time Mum had actually said it out loud.

'I understand that you will leave as soon as you can,' she said, her eyes dropping again as she wiped at the corners of them and sniffed. 'I don't blame you. I would do the same. But . . . I will miss you.'

Matt stepped across the hallway and gave his mum a hug. It was getting to be a habit. 'I don't want to leave *you*,' he said. 'Just him. You know . . . I don't even really want to join the Navy. I'd rather go on to college and study zoology; work with birds and animals.'

She nodded, smiling up at him. 'I see you with your bird,' she said. 'It is wonderful the way you communicate. You have a gift.'

Matt blinked. Mum had *seen* him with Lucky? 'She's a special bird,' he said, wondering if Mum knew *how* special. 'But Mum, the trouble is I can't stay here too much longer. You know that, don't you? You know if I do, one day, me and Dad . . .'

She nodded again. 'I know. Let me think about it. I may find an answer. But now . . . go to bed, *kochany*, before he gets back. He may have drunk too much.'

'Mum,' said Matt, pausing in his bedroom doorway. 'Would you cover for me . . . with Dad . . . if it was really important?'

Mum looked worried, pushing her straight dark hair off her creased brow. 'I will always cover for you if I can, you know that. What do you need me to do?'

'I . . . I'll let you know,' said Matt, retreating into his room. 'And . . . Mum.'

She smiled at him.

'I love you.'

Her smile twisted and she sniffed and then nodded and went away to her room.

Matt sat on his bed, waiting. Every moment that passed

brought him closer to the sound of Dad's key in the front door. He needed to get into the red metal box which sat behind the armchair in the living room. This was where all the important family documents were kept. Was Mum in bed yet? Would she wander out to the bathroom and overhear him riffling through the files? It was a risk he had to take. He got up, eased his door open, and trod quietly into the lounge.

The box gave a muffled clang as he unlatched it and he held his breath but heard no movement. With his pen torch gripped between his teeth, he found the passports file and unearthed his own. His photo was an embarrassment, taken two years ago when he was thirteen and his hair was still long and floppy. Matt pocketed it, closed the box file without further clanging, and crept back to his room.

At his bedside table he wrote Mum a note.

Dear Mum

If the parole officer calls for me, please say I've got flu or something. I won't be away for long and I promise you it's for a really, really important reason. Please take care of yourself . . . and Dad. The world might go a bit crazy in the next few days but I think it will be OK. I will try to explain when I'm back.

Love Matt
x

He gathered a few extra things in his backpack; a change of underwear, a baseball cap, some sun lotion, sunglasses, shorts, about £25 in cash that he'd saved up, which he zipped into a secure part of the bag with the passport. He put the bag over his shoulders, switched off his bedside lamp, and went to the wardrobe to get the escape ladder.

Lucky was waiting on his windowsill, as if she knew. He'd sent her home to roost after they'd rescued Carra, wanting her to get some sleep. 'It's good to see you,' he murmured, stroking her yellow beak. 'Is the coast clear? Can I get down?'

Lucky did a quick flight around the street and then alighted back on the sill and said: 'Clear.'

Matt dropped the rope ladder down the wall, slung his leg across the sill, and climbed down. At the bottom he pulled the cord, realizing as he watched the rope ladder concertina back up to the window, that his secret would be blown when Mum came in to find his note the next morning. The evidence of his escape would be pretty clear. Dad would probably spontaneously combust with rage when he found out. He just hoped poor Mum wouldn't take too much of the brunt of it. Although Dad never seemed to hit her, she had to manage so much of his rage it wore her out.

He turned to step out into the street when there was a sudden sweep of light and Matt threw himself behind the trunk of the birch tree just a second before a car turned onto the forecourt. His heart was pounding somewhere under his chin as he watched his father stagger out of a taxi, pay the driver, and then turn towards the steps up to the flat, burping gently and humming a song.

Just go, Dad – just go, keep going! chanted a small, scared voice in his head. The last thing he needed now, of all times, was a run in with his dad. Although it wouldn't stop him. It *couldn't* stop him.

Dad paused, swaying, on the other side of the tree. There was a clink. Dad swore. He'd dropped his keys. Matt saw, to his horror, that they'd fallen about a metre away from his hiding place. When Dad bent over and reached to pick them up, he would surely see his son flattened up against the trunk.

Suddenly there was a shudder of feathers and a starling dropped down, seized the key ring in its beak, and flew across to the foot of the steps before dropping it with another clink.

'Well, wadabou*dat?*' burbled his father in wonder. He stared up as the bird flitted away, shook his head, burped again, and then picked up the key ring and went upstairs.

Matt didn't wait to watch his father trying to stab at the lock with his key; he slid around the tree and fled along the dark street, laughing in a slightly hysterical way.

CHAPTER 17

' . . . solar flare is thought to have been the culprit but the National Air Traffic Services centre at Swanwick has assured passengers that it has corrected the satellite issues and is operating as normal, in line with other national air traffic control centres around the world.'

The newsreader on BBC News 24 sounded calm and professional. If the media had got a hold of the true story there was no sign of it in the coverage. Until another full second had been knocked off the planet's rotation, most things would continue to work normally.

Stephen stared at his notes. His meeting was seven hours away and he still had no idea what to suggest to the Prime Minister once he'd delivered his bombshell. What action could you take against the *world slowing down?* How could you reverse it when you had no idea what was causing it? How could you plan to protect the population from threats on a scale nobody had ever imagined?

It would probably be appreciated by the government if he were to tip them off that most of London might be under water in a week or two. Give them a chance to relocate to the Peak District.

He had nothing for them—not even an explanation. *Something on the dark side of the moon?* That sounded so fanciful. Ridiculous. But then, so did the events of the past two days— the tidal anomalies, the air traffic control glitch . . . and then the dancing squirrels and the singing husky.

Perhaps he had gone mad? This seemed like a very sweet possibility for a few moments. Then Stephen picked up his phone and tapped up the Hickson girl's number. Was he *really* desperate enough to phone a teenage girl in the middle of the night in hopes she might have an answer for him?

Turns out, yes. He hit CALL and waited, willing himself not to sound scared and needy. The call was picked up quickly but with an older voice. 'Elena's phone,' it said. 'Hi Stephen.'

'Is that Callie?'

'Yes, Elena's just upstairs packing.'

'Packing? Where is she going?'

'We're all going to Dubai,' said Callie. 'Me, Elena, Matt, and Carra.'

Steve rubbed his face. The woman sounded so normal she had to be mad.

'Matt is Elena's friend who can talk to birds and Carra is an alien who's come to help,' went on Callie, sounding positively certifiable.

'Can . . . can the alien . . . help?' he heard himself ask.

'We hope so. But we have to get to the tallest tower in the world to find out.'

'I see,' he said, as if he did.

'There's an alien spacecraft on the dark side of the moon,' she added.

'Of course there is.'

There was a pause and then Callie said: 'We're not leaving for a while yet. Do you want to come over and meet Carra?'

'NO!' he should have said. 'Don't be ridiculous. I am preparing for a breakfast meeting with the Prime Minister!'

Instead he said: 'Yes. Yes I do.' And five minutes later he was on the road to Thornleigh.

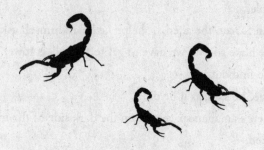

CHAPTER 18

Tima woke up at 4.34 a.m. exactly. She sat up in the hotel room bed, checked the bedside clock, and instinctively glanced up as if the beam was whooshing through. And it was . . . 3,400 miles away in Thornleigh.

Back in the UK it was 1.34 a.m. Here, it was three hours later and the only whooshing came from the hotel air conditioning.

She picked up her phone and called Elena. The bill would be astronomical and she'd be in such trouble with Mum and Dad when it came through . . . but right now she would *love* to know that something like a big phone bill would still matter a month from now.

Elena picked up on the third, weird, international ring. 'Tima. Are you OK?'

'Yes!' hissed Tima, aware that the connecting door between her room and her parents' room wasn't too thick. 'I just woke up as the beam came through—even though it doesn't come through here!'

'It's habit,' said Elena. 'It's like it's in our DNA now. Yes . . .' she went muffled, speaking to someone else, ' . . . it's gone now. No . . . I think only me, Matt, and Tima can feel it and hear it. And sort of see it.' The muffle went away. 'Sorry, Tee—I had Mum and Dr Steve come up to my room with Matt, Carra, and Spin, in case they could pick up the beam. They can't really, although Mum thinks she got goosebumps as it came through.'

Tima felt awed and not a little envious. 'Does your Mum know *everything* now?'

'Pretty much,' said Elena. 'As much as I've had time to tell her, anyway.'

'Wow,' said Tima. 'And she hasn't had you committed to a funny farm?!'

Elena gave a short sigh. '*Mental health unit*,' she corrected. 'No. Mum's spent enough time there herself. She doesn't fancy getting her daughter sectioned too!'

'And what about this scientist? Is he going to call the authorities and get you all locked up?'

'Right now he's more interested in talking to Carra about wormholes and dark matter,' said Elena.

Tima shook her head, imagining the weirdest house party ever at the end of this phone call. 'So . . . are you coming?' She got out of bed and padded across the thick carpet to gaze out into the pre-dawn light of Dubai.

'Yes,' said Elena. 'We're on the 7.05 a.m. flight from Stansted. We get in around five o'clock Dubai time. We might be able to make it to the tower before seven. Can you get there too?'

'I'm working on that,' said Tima, nibbling on a fingernail and eyeing the needle-like silhouette of the Burj Khalifa on the horizon. In truth, she was *some way off* figuring out a way to reach it; somehow escaping her parents and finding her way alone to meet her friends was a tricky little challenge. But she had a few hours yet, to come up with a plan.

'Problem is,' she went on. 'Spin's been talking about getting up 828 metres . . . but I don't think that's going to happen. I mean . . . that's the *top* of the tower. None of the tours will let you go that high. The highest you can get is to the restaurant on the 148th floor. And there are 163 floors, not including the spire access levels.'

Elena sighed. 'OK. Well . . . we'll have to work something out. Tima—just get there, OK? We need you.'

'Do you? Maybe you only need Carra?' said Tima, although she hated to think she might be left out.

'No,' said Elena. 'All of us. You, me, Matt, and Carra. We *all* need to be there. Carra says we do but even if she hadn't, I *know* it. We all go.'

'It'll be like old times,' said Tima. 'Except without Spin. I guess he's *not* coming.'

'No,' said Elena. 'He can't.'

'Good to have someone back in Thornleigh,' said Tima. 'Does he have a phone? Will he let you have his number?'

'I don't think he really *does* that kind of thing,' said Elena. 'But I'll ask.'

'OK . . . well . . . I'd better get back to bed,' said Tima. 'I'll see you all at the Burj in the evening. Stay in touch.'

After the call she stayed at the window, staring at the tower for a long time. She had already tried to talk Mum and Dad into an evening visit to the Burj but it turned out they were all going to have dinner with her aunt and cousins that night, so Mum had said they'd have to go another time. Tima sighed. She loved her parents and hated to do it . . . but she was going to have to cheat and deceive them . . . and probably worry them sick.

She went to listen at the connecting door. Beyond it she could hear the occasional low snore from her father but nothing else. Up on the 19th storey of the hotel, with its sealed windows and climate control, there were few insects or spiders to call on for guidance, but she was pretty sure Mum and Dad were fully asleep. Tima took a deep breath and slowly opened the door. It made no sound as she stepped through and into her parents' room. By the dim light shining through the curtains she navigated to the dressing table where Mum kept her bag and dipped her hand inside it to find Mum's wallet of credit cards.

Her hand closed on the cool leather instantly, sending both relief and regret bouncing through her nervous system. If she hadn't found the wallet she could have abandoned this plan.

She slipped back into her room with her guilty prize, closing the door silently behind her, and then found the Burj Khalifa ticket booking site on her phone. She bagged herself a ticket that would go as high as the restaurant level; it wasn't cheap and she winced as she entered the last number from Mum's card and hit PAY. The e-ticket—for 8 p.m. entry, in case the others were late—was texted back to her phone; she didn't even need to print it off.

Next she searched for a local taxi firm. The online booking system was a godsend, because she didn't need to talk to anyone and try to sound older than eleven. She put in the address of her cousin's house and entered the collection time. In the extra guidance section she wrote: PLEASE DO NOT KNOCK OR RING AT THE HOUSE. TEXT MESSAGE ME ON YOUR ARRIVAL.

She paid in advance and then, filled with a gut-churning mix of guilt, dread, and excitement, stealthily returned the wallet to Mum's bag. Safely back in her own room she told herself: *I might not go. There might be another solution. The Ayotian ship could just go away in the night . . . you never know.*

It would be a first.

She lay down on the carpet and stretched out one hand, palm up. Turned out she *did* have some company after all. A small black spider with a red hourglass on its abdomen wandered across the carpet and onto her palm. Anyone else would have been screaming by now, the redback being one of the country's most venomous arachnids. But Tima knew she was safe. She missed Spencer, the house spider who shared her bedroom back home. This substitute might help her relax.

'Hi Ruby,' she said. 'Can I tell you about my worries . . . ?'

Ruby settled in the middle of her palm and got ready to listen.

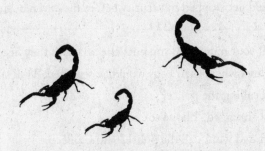

CHAPTER 19

If it wasn't for the whole 'end of the world' thing, Elena would have been having a lovely time. She and Mum had never flown abroad before; there had never been enough money.

Well, she *had* been on a plane twice when she was younger, before Dad left, but that was only a quick hop over to Jersey for a holiday—and back again. The airport was vast and exciting as she, Mum, Carra, and Matt made their way to check-in. They had no hold luggage to stow; they'd all agreed to travel light, with just a backpack each. It cost a lot less and they could get away in Dubai that much faster, not having to wait around for cases to come off the plane.

Matt was quiet. Elena could guess how he felt. He was on probation. Although the terms of his suspended sentence hadn't mentioned anything about not leaving the country, as soon as his parents found out he was missing, there could be an alert. Matt could get stopped by security before they even boarded the plane.

'Will your mum help you out?' she asked, as they headed into the area where their bags would be searched. 'Will she stop your dad calling the police?'

Matt shrugged. 'I hope so.'

'Your dad won't call the police,' said Callie.

Matt glanced at her. 'How do you know?'

'Because he won't want them to know you've absconded. Not until he has to. I mean, it's really lucky for him that the local paper wasn't covering your court case, or it'd be all over the news—and that could damage the carwash business.'

'True,' said Matt, nodding.

'So he's not going to call the cops on you and risk another court appearance, is he?'

Matt visibly relaxed a notch. 'No . . . You could be right.'

'I am right,' said Callie. 'When's your next litter picking trip?'

'Wednesday,' said Matt.

'So—nothing to worry about for a couple of days,' said Callie. 'Matt—you are doing the only thing you *can* do right now, for your mum and your dad . . . and everyone. None of us have a choice. So stop worrying about what's happening at home. We've got bigger things to deal with.'

Elena held her breath as Matt was called through passport control and on to the bag check. At every point she expected a siren to go off.

Carra strode through without a twitch, despite the fact that she didn't even belong on the *planet*, let alone to the United Kingdom. Her alien tech, laid out on a plastic tray and rolling through the sensor machines, seemed to pass for Earth tech; at least none of the security staff gave it a second glance. Happily, her inhaler, in her bag, also escaped suspicion. It didn't look much like an ordinary asthma inhaler, but Carra needed it. If she didn't use it twice a day, Earth's mix of gases could eventually kill her.

When the siren *did* go off, it was for *Elena*—but only because she'd forgotten to chuck away a bottle of water in her bag. The security woman gave her a weary raised eyebrow and dropped the offending bottle in a bin and then they were free to wander through to airside and find the gate their plane would depart from.

'I hope we are not delayed,' said Carra, as they found some seats looking out onto the runway.

'Me too,' said Elena. 'We need to get there in time to meet Tima.'

'That is not my concern,' said Carra, examining her wrist gadget. 'We will reach a further second of delay in Earth's revolution a short while after we take off. The satellite systems will glitch again.'

Elena gulped. 'While we're *up* there?'

'It will be worse if we're not up there,' said Carra. 'Planes may be grounded. But if we are already flying then there will be time for the glitch to be resolved before we land in Dubai.'

Elena nodded, feeling waves of nervous anxiety buffeting her.

'It'll be *fine*,' said Callie, stretching and yawning. 'Everyone, just chill out.'

'Whatever your mum takes,' muttered Matt, 'I'd like some.'

'Me too,' said Elena. She hoped never to need drugs of any kind to live a normal life, but right now, she and a runaway with a criminal record, a mother with bipolar disorder, and an alien with significant breathing issues were planning to fly across the planet in hopes of scaling the world's tallest tower to put out a signal to save mankind. Things were far from normal.

The flight was not delayed. Half an hour later they were boarding. As they walked along the covered bridge to the cabin door, there was a sudden rapping sound.

'Will you look at *that?*' said an American traveller. 'Is it an English woodpecker?'

Matt spun around and ran to the curved window—the last view outside before he boarded. Clinging to a ridge of metal on the outer side was Lucky. She had followed them all the way to Stansted and was now tapping to get Matt's attention.

'Lucky . . . you can't come!' he said, pressing his hand to the glass. 'I'm sorry!'

Elena squeezed his shoulder. 'She'll be OK,' she said. 'She probably understands. She just wanted to say goodbye.'

Matt laid his forehead against the transparent barrier and closed his eyes as fellow travellers streamed past them, some casting curious glances at the boy and the bird which was pressing *its* forehead against the far side. Elena couldn't tell what Matt was saying to Lucky in his head, but it made her throat tighten and her eyes well up to watch them.

Then Lucky suddenly flitted away and it was over. They moved on through the walkway. Matt, obviously more upset than he looked, dropped his boarding pass at the cabin door and spent some time scrabbling for it on the floor. Then, at last, they were all on board, Elena sitting at the window, next to Mum, and Matt sitting alongside Carra in the aisle seats. Matt looked happier as he carefully stowed his bag under the seat in front.

Carra raised a dark eyebrow at him. 'Was that wise?'

'I don't care,' said Matt.

Which was when Elena realized that Lucky was hiding in his backpack. She recalled how Matt had dropped his boarding pass and scrabbled on the floor . . . right by the gap where the airbridge reached the plane. A gap big enough for a clever starling to squish through.

She grinned across at Matt, shaking her head. 'Better hope you can do the same trick at the other end!'

The surprises didn't end there. Shortly before the cabin doors were due to close there was a late arrival, puffing into the cabin and apologizing for holding everyone up.

It was Dr Stephen Baxendale.

CHAPTER 20

If it wasn't for that bright pink neon *THE END IS NIGH* sign buzzing on and off in the back of her mind, Tima would have been having a great holiday.

She and her parents had spent most of the day on an Arabian Desert safari, along with her aunt and uncle and her cousin Zaria. Zaria was a year older than Tima and although they'd only met a handful of times on family holidays, they got on well.

They'd all been taken out into the desert in a big four-wheel drive vehicle and spent a couple of hours wildlife spotting.

'We've *never* had a day like this!' said Lohi, the Indian tour guide, dropping his binoculars from his eyes to stare at them all in astonishment as they stood at the top of a golden dune. 'Snake eagle, sooty falcon, lappet-faced vulture . . . oryx, desert hedgehogs . . . even a sand cat!' He paused, counting through their encounters on his fingers. 'And a sand boa, a horned viper, a saw-scaled viper . . .'

'Don't forget the feral goats,' added Louisa, the super fit South African dune driver, who'd told them she'd trained for months to manage the slippery dunes in a four-wheel drive tourist vehicle.

'It's been brilliant!' said Tima, smiling brightly.

'Brilliant?! It's been *amazing*,' said Mum. 'It's like they've all been lined up, waiting for us!'

'They just keep on coming,' said Zaria, shaking her head in wonder.

'If we see a spiny mouse,' said Lohi, 'I will *know* this is a dream.'

Tima took a deep breath and told herself to stop. Something about the clear, hot desert air seemed to have carried her communications with the local wildlife far and wide. She had never expected them all to be so obliging. She was slightly disappointed in the lack of scorpions, but she knew these were nocturnal, so she hadn't really expected to see any in the day and she had stopped short of asking them. They'd be extra vulnerable to birds and snakes if they came out by daylight.

'So,' said Louisa, as the 4x4 rolled to a stop near a whitewashed building with a roof of salmon pink clay tiles. 'How would you like to travel to your lunch by camel?'

Everyone made excited noises, although Mum looked a bit uneasy. 'Don't they spit?' she said.

'Not as much as they fart,' said Louisa, which got a big

laugh.

'Our camels are very used to visitors,' said Lohi. 'You do not need to worry. It is a very comfortable way to travel.'

He wasn't wrong. Four dromedaries were waiting for them in the shade of the building, attended by two men who were to be their guides on the trek. Each camel had a colourful fabric saddle attached just behind its hump. After checking that their guests had hats on and had applied sun cream to their arms and the backs of their necks, the guides made the camels kneel. Tima, it turned out, was to ride the same camel as Mum—Zaria got on with *her* mother.

'Aren't we too heavy—both of us?' Mum asked.

'They're fine,' said Tima, immediately aware of how strong her camel was and how little concerned about its passengers. 'Whoooaaah!' Everyone clung on to handles in the saddles as their camels suddenly got to their feet. It was thrilling to feel the easy, swinging movement of these long-limbed creatures as they began to lope across the sand towards a distant oasis where lunch was being laid on.

Is this OK? Tima sent to her camel, as she was rocked gently across the dunes, the warmth of its furry hump permeating through the cloth saddle and her light summer trousers. *Do you mind?*

The camel sent back that it did not mind *her*. Sometimes it minded passengers who were heavy or panicky or smelt bad.

Tima laughed out loud. The camel smelt pretty *rich* itself. *But you're lovely*, she added, in case it had caught that thought and was insulted. The camel paused, and turned its head right around to look at her. It *was* lovely, with thick long lashes around liquid brown eyes and a soft, mobile mouth. It was taking a moment to study *her*. Clearly it had never met a Night Speaker before.

By the time they'd reached the oasis (a small hotel complex, in fact, with palm trees, courtyard gardens, and a pool), Tima had decided she was a big fan of camels. She wished Elena was here to meet this one, and then realized, with a thud in her belly, that Elena *would* be here in the Emirates in just a few hours.

After the animals had knelt and allowed them all to dismount, Tima went around to rest her brow against their camel's forehead. The guide was anxious. 'Careful . . . she can spit,' he warned.

'She won't,' said Tima, stroking the creature's big, velvety nose. 'Have you noticed her ear is sore?'

The guide frowned. 'Where?' he asked.

'Some way in,' said Tima. 'It's hurting her a bit. Might be an abscess.'

'Oh,' said the guide, now peering closely into the camel's left ear. 'It *is* sore. How did you *know* that . . . ?' he called after her, as she went to join the others.

'My mum's a vet,' she called back, which seemed to satisfy him.

In the cool shade of the courtyard, the party was served with a spicy dish called Mutton Ghoozi, rice, and roasted vegetables, followed by stuffed dates and a sweet rice pudding.

'Fit for a king,' murmured Tima as she sat beside the pool with Zaria. 'I could get used to this.'

'All you need to do is marry a sheikh,' said Zaria. 'Or be one.'

'Not sure I'll ever want to do the marrying thing,' said Tima. 'I'll have to be one instead.' She chuckled, imagining herself as one of the wealthy men she'd seen in this country. They all seemed very serious and important in the way they walked. They were usually dressed in kandoras—long white shirt things which skimmed their ankles—and ghutra on their heads; soft white scarves crowned with a kind of thin doughnut of black fabric called an agal. Tima thought they looked rather elegant. She wasn't sure *she* could pull it off, though.

She liked the women's fashion too. Aside from those dressed from head-to-toe in black, some women wore western clothes under long lightweight black coats, called abayas, with fine black headscarves called shaylas. Others wore long-sleeved, full-length dresses known as jalabiyas. These were often in dazzling colours, many trimmed with beads, crystals, and exquisite golden embroidery. None of it would work for her night-time adventures, though . . .

'I'd love to be rich here,' said Zaria. 'It's an amazing life. All the royals and their friends are into horse racing and falconry. Arabs love their horses and falcons. It's a big thing here. And extreme sports—lots of them go in for sailing and flying and sky-diving.'

Sitting here, bathed in golden sunshine, chatting with her cousin in this beautiful place, Tima could almost forget the threat hanging over them. She could almost believe that it wasn't real. After all . . . what evidence had *she* seen? None.

'It's a bit busy up there, isn't it?' said her Uncle Khalid, who'd been talking to Mum and Dad as they shared stuffed dates. Tima followed his gaze and felt her world shake once again.

White circles were scrawled across the deep blue sky. Roaming lazily among them were at least seven aeroplanes, all at different heights, adding more vapour trails to the picture.

'Must be a problem at the airport,' said Louisa, the dune driver. She flicked on her smartphone and began surfing the news feeds. 'Yeah—looks like there's a big air traffic control issue.'

Again? Tima closed her eyes and breathed slowly, trying to steady her suddenly rapid heartbeat. She had *nearly* convinced herself that the Earth had stopped slowing, just as mysteriously as it had begun. Even with everything she'd heard from the others about that Ayotian ship, a part of her just refused to believe it. But now this. Elena had said they thought there might be another air traffic control glitch while they were flying over. The rate of deceleration had obviously gone into its second second, and thrown out the satellite clocks once again.

'Don't look so worried, darling,' said Mum, noticing her face. 'I'm sure the planes won't start dropping into the desert! They'll all be landing soon. Here—try these pistachio-stuffed dates. They are *amazing*.'

CHAPTER 21

'Ladies and gentlemen,' said the pilot, through the 747's PA system. 'Good news—the problem at Dubai Airport has been resolved and I'm pleased to tell you that we are at last able to land.'

There was a cheer among the passengers, who'd been getting more and more tense as their flight had repeatedly circled above the coastal city. You could even get tired of looking down at the palm-tree-shaped manmade island after two hours, thought Matt. And how much fuel was left in this 747?

He'd sneaked a few berries from his onboard dessert into the backpack where Lucky was hiding, feeling more and more guilty about allowing her to come. She'd been cramped up inside for well over nine hours and he was really worried about her. Earlier he'd carefully wiped the salt off his inflight peanuts and fed her a number of them. He guessed there would be a fair bit of starling poo inside the backpack and hoped she'd aimed for his plastic washbag rather than his fleece.

At last they were able to make their weary way along the aisle and down onto the airbridge. The scientist guy, who'd told them all to just call him Steve rather than Dr Baxendale, fell into step with Elena's mum and Carra, while Matt and Elena followed on behind.

'I'm a bit freaked out,' admitted Elena, staring around her at the impressive architecture of the airport with its decorative pillars and fountains. 'Are you a bit freaked out?'

'Yeah, I'm a bit freaked out,' he agreed. 'But mostly I just want to set Lucky free.'

This wasn't easy. There had been no gaps in the tunnel from the plane to the air-conditioned terminal. Matt began to seriously worry. He couldn't let Lucky out until he was certain she could fly safely . . . and getting through passport control was a big concern. What if they had to put their bags through another scanning machine?

'I can't see any open windows, can you?' he said.

Elena shook her head. 'Don't worry—we'll find a way.'

The way, when it came, was quite simple. There were large fig trees planted in massive pots. As they approached the part of the concourse where everyone began to queue with their passports at the ready, the area beyond the barriers could be seen. There were more potted trees on the other side. It looked as if they were placed decoratively every twenty metres or so, right out to the exit.

'Get Lucky into this tree,' whispered Elena. 'Then tell her to fly across the barrier to the next tree, over there.' She pointed. 'She can flit from tree to tree as we head out. She should be fine.'

Matt nodded, slightly annoyed at himself for not working this out before Elena. They stood close to the tree and pretended they were looking at something on Elena's phone for a minute, while Matt gently eased open the top of his bag and Lucky, with obvious relief, hopped out of it and into the branches of the fig tree. She shuddered her feathers and began to preen furiously.

'See you on the other side,' muttered Matt.

'Other side,' repeated Lucky.

'Shhhh,' said Matt, glancing around anxiously. 'No speaking here! You're under cover.'

Lucky didn't comment further. Reluctantly Matt walked on with Elena, catching up with the adults. They were an odd bunch—Callie, blonde and smiling and remarkably lively after their epic flight, Steve, tall and broad with dark grey hair, also looking unfeasibly bright.

Perhaps it was because they were in deep conversation with an alien. Carra might look human but she was from another galaxy. Maybe another *dimension*. This was probably why Steve had blown out his meeting with the Prime Minister. He couldn't bear to miss the chance for more discussion with Carra, about life, the universe, and everything.

'. . . how many civilizations do you know of?' Steve was asking as he and Elena caught up and queued behind them.

'And how did you all work out the corridor thing?' Callie added. 'Is it all to do with black holes and dark matter?'

'Your scientists have got quite a lot right but some things entertainingly wrong,' Carra was saying. 'If we can stop your planet's imminent catastrophe, I may be able to give you some answers—although I am restricted by Quorat Protocol Twelve.'

'What's that?' asked Steve.

'I am only allowed to reveal as much as is safe and wise to a newly-acquainted life form.'

Matt blinked and shook his head. Sometimes he really wondered how he had come to be where he was, with these people, at this time. The beam. That was the answer. If he'd slept in a different room at home he would never have become a Night Speaker. He checked his watch. It was about four o'clock in the afternoon back in the UK; he wondered how Mum was coping with his disappearance . . . and with Dad. She would never in a million years dream that her son had upped and flown to Dubai.

There was a slight flicker and he glanced up in time to see Lucky flit over his head and alight in a fig tree on the far side of the barrier. Nobody else seemed to have noticed. He breathed out.

'Um . . . has anyone checked how late the Burj Khalifa stays open?' said Elena, bringing the science talk to a stop with more pressing matters.

'Until 10 p.m.,' said Callie. 'We should make it for the 9 p.m. entry if we get a cab now.'

They got through passport control with no issues, although Matt was convinced someone would suddenly slap a hand on his shoulder and demand to know what he thought he was doing.

Of course, to the casual observer they probably looked like a normal family group. Callie and Steve could be his mum and dad. Elena could be his sister and Carra . . . well, Carra could be their rather glamorous cousin.

A few seconds before they reached the sliding doors to the outside world, Matt held up his fist and Lucky alighted on it. Matt could see security staff by the door, so he stowed Lucky inside his bag again before she could be seen. Her small body thrummed against his fingers and he realized she was as excited as he was to be in this foreign land. Outside, the warmth of the evening air took his breath away.

Steve took charge, finding a large taxi that could carry them all and asking to travel to the Burj Khalifa right away. The driver was concerned about the destination he'd been asked for. After a rapid discussion with an airport worker he turned to Steve. 'No . . . no cases? No hotel?' he checked, in thickly-accented English.

'It's OK—we're meeting some friends at the tower,' said Matt. 'Then we'll be going on to the hotel afterwards. We're travelling light.'

The driver looked surprised. 'You speak Urdu?' He beamed widely. 'Most unusual in people from Britain.'

'I, er, have a friend from . . .' Matt began, wondering where to go with his explanation; he'd only just picked up the man's native tongue after hearing him speak to the airport worker and had no idea where he was from.

'. . . Pakistan, like me?' said the taxi driver, helpfully. 'Excellent. Very excellent.'

Matt realized that Steve and Callie were staring at him,

opened-mouthed. Elena was grinning while Carra was just climbing into the front seat, next to the driver.

'It's a Night Speaker thing,' explained Elena, as they got into the back of the people carrier. 'We can communicate with any living thing. Including humans from anywhere on the planet.'

'You . . . you're fluent in Arabic?' murmured Steve.

'Well, that was actually Urdu, but we're fluent in everything,' said Elena, shrugging. 'Well, so far . . . We don't even know we're doing it. We just hear someone speak their language and we know it. It's been . . . awkward at times.'

Steve shook his head. 'Astonishing. And you believe this beam of yours . . . that's what caused this?'

'Yeah,' said Matt, getting Lucky out but keeping her low on his fist. 'Tima got her head scanned. They found that her . . . what are they called?'

'Angular gyri,' supplied Elena.

'Yeah—the angular gyri—the bits in the brain that are for speech and communication—they're massively bigger and more active in her brain. So we reckon we're the same.'

'Just astonishing . . .' Steve looked from Elena to Matt and back again. 'Like meeting an alien wasn't quite enough.'

Matt shrugged. 'Carra's cool. You should see her when she's angry, though.'

'Would you . . . I mean . . . if we all get through this, would you allow me to scan your brains?' asked Steve.

Matt and Elena exchanged glances. They'd been keeping their secret for so long, it wasn't an easy thing to agree to.

'Let's just get to the tower and see if we can save the planet first, OK?' said Elena.

'Fair enough,' said Steve.

'Is Tima already there?' asked Matt.

Elena checked her phone and shook her head. 'I've been trying not to stress out about it . . . but I haven't heard from Tima in *hours*.'

'That,' said Steve, checking his own phone, '. . . is because the mobile networks have gone down.'

CHAPTER 22

'The network has gone down!' Her taxi driver rapped at his satnav with his knuckles and swore under his breath.

'Are you sure?' asked Tima, slipping into his language instantly, so he glanced back at her, embarrassed. He'd obviously had her down as a Brit, not expecting her to be fluent in his own tongue.

'Sorry, miss,' he said, looking abashed. 'But . . . yes. My satnav is down and my phone maps aren't working.'

'But you know your way to the Burj, yes?'

'Oh yes,' he nodded. 'It is fine. I was checking for my next job, after I drop you off. And I was surprised.'

'Maybe there's something about it on the radio?' asked Tima, gulping back her nerves. As if this whole evening wasn't terrifying enough! She had slipped away from her cousin's house, leaving everyone talking at the dinner table. She had simply sidled quietly out of the room, walked down the hall, out through the front door, jumped into a taxi and gone. She had *never* done something as bold and badly behaved as this before. She hadn't left Mum and Dad a note. She'd planned to drop them a text to let them know she was OK. She hadn't even worked out what she was going to say. What possible excuse could she give?

And now she couldn't give *any* excuse, because the mobile networks were down. With a groan she noticed her last two texts to Elena sitting, unsent, in her messages list with little exclamation marks next to them.

Are you OK up there? We can see planes stacking up?

And then:

Text me as soon as you land. I will be at the Burj by 8 p.m. at the latest.

Nothing from Elena either, of course; Tima had no idea whether her plane had even landed yet.

'Can you put the radio on?' she asked the driver. 'There might be news.'

The driver sighed and said: 'If the radio stations are working!'

A few of the preset buttons he pressed led only to an ominous hissing, but eventually he found a local Dubai-based station which was probably broadcasting via an old style transmitter, Tima guessed. The bigger ones using satellites were all off-air. In the last ten minutes before she was dropped off, Tima at least learned that planes *were* now landing and the backlog was slowly being dealt with. And yes—all the mobile phone networks across the country were down. In fact, said the rather excitable presenter, it might be all over the *world!*

'What is going on with this world?' asked the driver, shaking his head. 'Cybercrime!'

Tima smiled weakly and muttered: 'I *wish* . . .'

'Are you OK here?' asked the driver as he pulled into the drop-off point for visitors to the tower. It was dusk now and the shopping mall at its base was lit up and twinkling like Christmas. Many Emiratis chose to shop in the cool of the evening. 'Are you meeting someone?' the driver persisted. 'Where are they?'

Tima was touched by his concern—and worried. 'I'm meeting my mother,' she said, quickly. She could see a dark-haired woman in western clothes standing by the glass doors to the mall, looking at her phone. 'There she is!' she improvised. 'Thank you so much.'

'No problem, go safely!' he replied, getting out to open the door for her before she could do it herself. He stood, solicitously watching her as she walked to the entrance to the mall. *Damn!*

Tima went up to the woman. 'Hi,' she said, with her widest smile. The woman, charmed, smiled warmly back. *Bingo!* 'Is your phone working?' Tima asked. 'I think there's a problem with the networks.'

'Yes—that's what I've heard too,' said the woman. 'I can't text or email or anything.'

Tima took the opportunity to step closer to her in a familiar way, showing off her own phone and its lack of connectivity. This was enough to convince the conscientious driver and at last he got back into his car and drove away.

'It'll probably be back up again any time,' said the woman. 'Are you OK? Are you meeting someone?'

Oh *great*. Not another concerned adult. Tima waved at someone inside the mall. 'Yes—there they are. Better go. Byeee.' And she ran into the building before she could worry anyone else. Honestly, she would be so relieved to grow a foot taller and not look so like a child.

Once inside the opulent shopping centre she quickly navigated her way along the marble floors, past impressive artworks and monolithic water features, to the entrance to the Burj Khalifa. Happily, she had saved her e-ticket as an image on her phone and did not rely on accessing her email to find it.

The network issues were causing a minor stir in the reception area of the tower as Tima walked with a small crowd along a curved corridor past images of the Burj rising from its foundations during construction. 'I can't get any signal at all,' said an American woman to her companion. 'What the hell's wrong with the network?'

'It's terrorists!' muttered a man who sounded French.

'It's a power outage,' suggested the American woman's companion, humorously. 'They all forgot to pay their bills!'

'It's aliens,' said Tima as she passed them. Everyone laughed.

A high-speed lift took her to the first level—erroneously named *At the Top* (it wasn't even two thirds of the way up). Once out of the lift she could see what everyone else was here for—a vast panorama of the city at dusk. Lights twinkled in every direction as the last of the sun's peachy rays filtered across the sea out west. Close up to the glass, the drop was dizzying, but Tima didn't have time to stop. For all she knew, everyone else was already here. She quickly toured the semi-circular floor with its open-air viewing platform and gift shop. None of her friends were here. Again and again she reached for her phone, only to see NO NETWORK blinking up in the corner of the screen.

It was time to go on up to the restaurant level. They were probably already there.

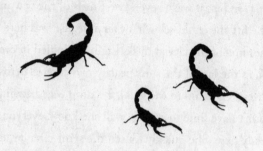

CHAPTER 23

'*How* much?' Callie gulped as they stood at the ticket desk. It had taken them so long to get here and everyone was exhausted; really only awake because of the almost electric thrill of finally reaching the world's tallest tower.

Elena took a deep breath. This could be very awkward. They didn't have much money left and almost no credit available on Mum's Mastercard. And now the ticket price to get them all even part way up the tower was in four figures! Of course, that was in the local currency, the dirham, but even when Mum and Steve calculated what it was in sterling, it was still in three figures . . . for all of them.

Carra was no help, standing and staring up as if she could see through all the floors above them with X-ray eyes, and Matt had only a few quid in sterling. What were they going to do?

'It's fine,' said Steve. 'I've got this.' And he magically produced a shining silver credit card to get them all a ticket to the Lounge level—as far up as tourists could go.

And then what? wondered Elena, not for the first time—although this was the first time she'd really *listened* to that inner voice. The highest Lounge level was still only floor 154 and there were 163 floors. Was floor 154 going to be high enough for Carra to communicate with her people?

'Um . . . there's a problem,' Steve was saying. The immaculate woman behind the ticket desk was looking apologetic.

'What's up?' said Matt, surreptitiously checking the small opening in his backpack where a yellow beak occasionally emerged. 'Can you still pay by card with the mobile networks down?'

'No—they have an old style backup system for that,' said Steve, indicating the paper dockets the reception team were using to record card numbers and take signatures.

'The problem is that they only have three spaces left,' said Callie. 'We might have to go ahead with Carra while you two wait down here.'

Elena, Matt, and Carra exchanged glances. Then Carra strode up to Callie and Steve and looked at them directly. 'I did not travel here to continue on with you,' she said, with her usual bluntness. 'I came here with Night Speakers. It is *you* who must wait below, not Elena and Matt.'

Elena saw her mother blush (a rare occurrence). 'Of course,' she said, nodding vigorously. 'I kind of forgot. Did the mum thing.'

Steve nodded too, looking disappointed. 'Fair enough,' he said. 'We'll wait here.'

'Could we all wait and go in half an hour or so?' wondered Callie, eyebrows raised hopefully.

'No—I'm sorry. I'm afraid there are no more spaces left this evening,' said the woman at the desk. 'The ten o'clock tour is full. Is that a *bird* in your bag?'

Matt laughed, quite convincingly, thought Elena. 'No,' he said. 'Just a toy for my kid brother.'

The reason the woman didn't pursue it was probably the security bag check around the next corner. Matt saw the machines and the uniforms and turned around to hand his bag to Callie with a sigh. 'Look after her until we get back down,' he said.

Then they went through security, got into the high-speed lift, and shot upwards as a video projection of the construction of the tower played around the walls and ceiling.

They got out and took a swift turn around the lower observation deck and gifts shop on level 148, in case Tima was there, and then went on up to the Lounge level.

As soon as the lift door opened Tima ran at them like a six-year-old, throwing her arms around them. 'Thank god you're *here!*' she squeaked.

Then she stepped back, took a look at Carra, and added 'Hi! Promise you don't want to kill me this time . . . ?'

Carra smiled. 'Today you are safe from me,' she said, before striding through the gleaming white and gold lobby towards the window view. 'It's other aliens you need to fear.'

'OK then,' said Tima, glancing from Elena to Matt. 'Now what?'

'Follow the extraterrestrial in green leather,' muttered Elena.

Carra had found the outdoor terrace. Everyone followed her outside where a dozen or so tourists were gazing down through the glass at the dizzying drop, most of them filming with their mobile phones. Tima had already been outside and taken in the view but Elena and Matt went straight to the glass to stare down at the world below. From here the city shimmered like a fairy tale mirage nestling against the Persian Gulf. Its many skyscrapers looked as if they'd been studded with twinkling gemstones. Through a mounted telescope, Elena could see more distant detail, including a line of white orbs glowing along the coastal promenades like a necklace of pearls. As the last gleam of the setting sun threw a violet light across the sea, the full moon was already rising. As she stepped back from the telescope and gazed up at it, Elena felt a prickling sensation across her skin. It could be just the knowledge of what was lurking on its dark side, but . . . she glanced at Matt and Tima. 'Are you . . . getting something?' she asked.

Tima shivered. 'I've been getting something for a little while. I thought it was just nerves. But . . . Matt?'

Matt was suddenly no longer looking down, but up at the top of the barrier, a metre above their heads. Elena blinked as she realized a large falcon was sitting on top of one of the security cameras, staring intently down at them.

'Yeah,' said Matt, drily. 'I'm getting something.'

Elena felt her shivers go up a notch. Of course, standing

here on the 152nd floor of the world's tallest building would be enough to give anyone the shivers. But this was something different—a sensation she had felt before when something *big* was about to happen. And not *big* in a good way.

'What's he telling you?' asked Tima, as a handful of the tourists noticed the raptor and turned their cameras in its direction.

'He's—what the *hell?*'

Matt stepped away from the falcon and stared up at the tower.

Carra was climbing it.

'Whaaaaat?' breathed Elena. Carra was doing a fair impression of Spiderman as she scaled the glass wall up to the floor above their terrace. She appeared to have something attached to her hands and feet—black circles which must have been . . . what? Suckers? Magnets?

'She *can't do that!*' hissed Tima, her brown eyes wide and round with horror.

'Yeah, but she *is* doing that,' muttered Matt.

Elena's heart was thudding wildly. She turned away, grabbing Tima and Matt's arms and spinning them away too. 'Don't look up any more,' she said. 'Maybe nobody will notice!'

And it did look as if that might work. Everyone was fixated either on the breathtaking view or the falcon still roosting on the security camera.

'She's got some crazy alien tech in that bag of hers!' muttered Matt as they joined the group of falcon watchers. 'How the hell did she get it through all the security machines?'

'She's running a baffler,' said Elena, trying to control her breathing and not feel quite so panicked. 'It's a gadget which throws up a kind of 4D mirage, making her stuff look like . . . other stuff. Normal stuff. Oh I really don't have a good feeling about any of this. She's crazy to climb up there—I can't bear to look. And something else is wrong. He knows it doesn't he?'

As if in response the falcon shifted its position, stared down hard at Matt, and then turned its gaze out to sea.

Elena followed the direction of its fierce stare. Something was bad . . . off-kilter. Her eyes scurried from left to right as her brain tried to tease out what was different about the view. She ran back to the telescope and pressed her eye to it. 'The pearls,' she muttered. 'I can't see the pearls!'

'What?' asked Tima, but before Elena could reply she was shaken almost out of her skin by the sudden shriek of an alarm siren.

At once there were shouts and a few screams from the tourists and then someone yelled: 'LOOK! Up there!'

'Ooh noooo,' wailed Tima, as everyone on the viewing platform—and a good number now spilling on to it—turned to stare up at Carra.

A Mexican wave of mobile phones rose to capture the spectacle of the woman attempting to climb the sheer face of the Burj Khalifa. Carra hadn't got very far. And she wasn't going to get much further.

Four uniformed security guards suddenly burst onto the scene with high powered torches which picked out the climber in dancing white spotlights. 'DO NOT MOVE! CLIMB

DOWN NOW! CLIMB DOWN NOW!' bellowed a voice. Elena gulped and clung on to her friends as she realized the white torches were attached to firearms.

'IF YOU DO NOT DESCEND IMMEDIATELY YOU WILL BE SHOT!' bellowed the chief security guard.

Elena quailed as she took in how this must look. Carra, dressed in her green leather, with her backpack on, clinging confidently to the side of the tower, looked pretty much exactly like a terrorist. The Burj was a natural target for terrorism. These men must be trained for just such an eventuality, here on the 152nd floor. What if they shot Carra? Right now? Then there would be NO HOPE for anyone on the planet.

She let go of Matt and Tima and ran forward, slipping instinctively into Arabic as she yelled: 'Please don't shoot! That's my friend! She's just a daredevil! She only wanted to take a selfie!'

Two of the men turned to her, guns still raised. Elena flung her hands up and did her best to look like a terrified kid. Which wasn't a stretch—she *was* a terrified kid.

Carra, thank god, had stopped climbing and was looking down at the crowd, her face lit brightly by the torches. She would be streaming live on all the social media feeds right now . . . if only the mobile networks were up and running.

'Tell her to come down!' demanded the security chief. 'RIGHT NOW!'

Elena dropped back into English as she yelled up: 'CARRA! Come DOWN. I'm sorry. We shouldn't have dared you! We didn't think you'd really do it!' And then, aware of Tima and Matt coming in close beside her, she burst into noisy tears.

'OK,' called down Carra. 'I'm coming down. Don't shoot.'

It took two or three painful minutes for Carra to descend, finally swinging down from the jut of the roof over the terrace. The moment she landed the security team was upon her, grabbing her raised arms and leading her back inside the building. Elena, Matt, and Tima raced after them. 'Where are you taking her?' demanded Tima in Arabic. 'What's going on?'

One of the team held back and addressed them all as the shrieking siren abruptly ceased. 'The police have been called,' he said, curtly. 'Your friend has broken the law and will be dealt with. You had better come with me.'

'My . . . our parents,' said Elena. 'They're waiting down at the entrance on the ground floor. We have to tell them what's happening.'

'We are going to the ground floor,' said the guard. 'Come now.'

All eight of them went into the lift. Carra was still being firmly held. She looked calm and resigned as the car began to descend at high speed. 'I am sorry,' she said. 'I did not want to cause alarm.'

The men holding her did not reply, but at least their firearms were now safely holstered. Elena's brain was buzzing like a fly in a bottle. What could they do now? If Carra was arrested there was no hope of getting her back up the tower.

'Look . . . do you *have* to call the police?' asked Tima, doing her best big-eyed charm. 'It's our fault . . . we dared her. We're meant to be going out for my birthday dinner now . . . and . . . and it's all going to be ruined.' Her eyes welled up and she began to sob, prettily. The men exchanged awkward glances but their chief was unmoved.

'The police have been called. You will have to have your birthday dinner without your friend,' he said. 'Or you may be held too. The crimes of trespass and reckless endangerment of life are very serious. And . . .' he glared pointedly down at Carra's wrists, which were still encircled in some kind of black climbing tech, '. . . I don't think this was a sudden decision, was it? It was planned.'

As soon as they emerged in the reception area, Elena ran ahead to her mother and Steve. 'Mum—Dad!' she said, widening her eyes meaningfully. 'Carra got into trouble! She tried to climb up the building for a dare.'

'Oh dear,' said Callie.

'Carra—what were you thinking of?' said Steve, stepping into his new role quickly.

'*Me and Matt are your kids and Tima and Carra are our friends,*' whispered Elena, as soon as she reached them.

The chief left Carra in the care of his team as he walked over to address the parents. 'Are you in charge of these children and this young woman?' he asked.

But before either of them could answer there was another interruption. Louder and somehow more frightening than the last, a new siren suddenly sounded. Everyone on reception seemed to jump. Several calls came through on the landline switchboard at once, and the series of monitors which had been showing non-stop imagery of the tower and its construction suddenly went blank and then showed Arabic lettering, which

Elena could not read.

The receptionists were losing their calm. And it was nothing to do with the incident up on the Lounge terrace. The chief went to the desk and spoke rapidly to someone on the phone and then gestured to his men to join him. They did so, hauling Carra along with them almost as an afterthought.

'It's serious,' said Elena. 'Something seriously bad is happening.'

Matt suddenly grabbed his bag from Callie and set Lucky free. 'Find out!' he said and the starling immediately flitted out through the glass entrance lobby into the mall.

'What's going on?' asked Steve, striding over to the reception desk, but the staff paid him no heed as they spoke to each other at high speed, their faces full of worry and ... yes ... fear.

Lucky was back with them two minutes later, landing on Matt's hand in full view of the Burj Khalifa employees who were now far too busy to notice; making calls and guiding visitors quickly out of the building, telling them there was an incident in the city and they needed to make their way to their homes or hotels as soon as possible. The strain of keeping the panic out of their voices was palpable, but they would not give anyone any details.

As Lucky landed Matt blinked and turned to face the others ... but Elena already knew.

'It's the coast, isn't it?' she said. 'I saw the lights on the promenade disappear.'

'Yes,' said Matt. 'They're under water. There's been a tidal surge. We have to get to the top of this building. We *have* to get Carra up there.'

'Not now, we don't,' said Steve. 'There's no chance right now. We need to get Carra away from here!'

It should have been a big, dramatic scene, grabbing Carra and getting out of there. But in the end it wasn't. Two guards had sat her down on a sofa and were now sitting on either side. Carra looked impassive and still and her captors paid scant attention to her as they strained to hear what was happening around them. Then, while her friends tried to work out what to do, the men suddenly sank quietly onto the soft seating and went to sleep.

Carra got up, stepped away from them, and walked over to join the others. The rest of the security team paid no attention at all as their trespasser and the family with her simply sidled out of the exit. 'What did you *do* to them?' breathed Elena.

'I have a spray to induce sleep,' said Carra. 'I carry it in my sleeve pocket. I let it off and held my breath until they were slumbering. It won't harm them. It will only last an hour or two—it was a small dose.'

Outside the air was filled with panic—and the cacophony of many sirens. Waving, Steve stepped out in front of another large taxi, making it screech to a halt.

The driver looked extremely worried. 'I go home,' he said. 'I'm sorry.'

'Is your home inland?' asked Steve. The driver nodded. 'Then please take us with you and drop us in a hotel along the way. I will pay double!'

The driver considered, glancing back over his shoulder as if expecting a tidal wave. 'It's OK,' Steve said. 'I'm a scientist—I specialize in oceans and tides. The sea won't come this far in.'

'OK—you get in,' agreed the driver, nodding vigorously, as if he might well appreciate having an expert in his cab.

Elena stared up at the tip of the Burj as the car pulled away and then closed her eyes. Getting Carra 828 metres up into the sky now looked like an impossible dream.

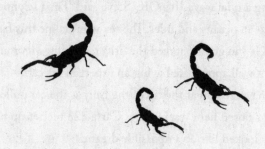

CHAPTER 24

It took a long time to get out of the city. The roads were clogged with panicky tourists heading one way and with emergency vehicles heading the other.

'They're not set up for this,' said Steve. 'There's no infrastructure to deal with flooding. They don't have high tides in this part of the world. Not until tonight.' He sighed, staring up at the moon. 'The variation here is little more than a metre on a normal day and they rarely have tidal surges so there's not much defence on the coast . . . of course so much of it is reclaimed for building . . . so that will make this anomaly worse. Most of Dubai is no more than six or seven metres above sea level.'

Tima wondered if he was talking to everyone or just to himself; he seemed to be feeling his way through his knowledge; thinking aloud.

'Do you know how high the water was?' asked Callie, who was sitting up front with the driver.

'Very high,' said the driver. 'Three . . . four metres. Cars floating. People swimming.' He switched on the radio and there was a cacophony of on-the-ground reporting, mostly in Arabic. Recordings of frightened people talking at speed played out in quick succession. 'We were in the car,' said one woman. 'And the water came up all around us and we were floating and the children were screaming. We were carried for maybe fifty metres and then we struck a building. We managed to scramble out onto the steps of the building.'

'The water rushed through the restaurant,' said a distraught-sounding man. 'My customers were yelling and getting onto the tables. What is happening?'

Tima gulped, wondering how her parents were coping. She got out her mobile and exclaimed: 'The network is back up!' There was a series of unanswered calls logged in her phone; all from Mum. Endless panicky texts too. Tima felt a wave of guilt wash over her. What could she say? In the end she just texted back:

SO sorry to scare you. I am OK. I am with Elena and Matt. I can't explain why just now but I will when I see you. Should be back tomorrow. Are you OK? Not flooded?

A second later her phone began to ring. Tima stared at it in panic.

'Best not,' said Elena, gently. 'Text back that you can't pick up calls. It'll be easier than trying to explain everything right now.'

Tima rejected the call and then texted:

Sorry—text only at the moment. I am FINE, I promise. Don't worry. Tell you everything tomorrow.

Then she did a photo of herself with Elena, both of them holding up their thumbs as if they were just on a cheeky girl's night out. She knew it was ridiculous but it should take down her parent's panic a notch.

'Best switch your phone off for a while now,' said Elena. 'They won't give up.'

Tima nodded. She caught her mother's return text:

This is crazy! What's going on? Why is Elena here? Are you caught up in the tidal surge? We are fine but please tell me where you are.

She took a deep breath and switched her phone off.

The driver dropped them at a small complex on the edge of the desert. 'You can stay here,' he said. 'It is not expensive.'

Steve produced his life-saving credit card and paid the man and then they all got out and stood, staring at a low whitewashed building with red tiles and a scraggy palm tree on either side of its arched front door. The building had seen better days but they didn't need five-star luxury. They just needed somewhere to rest for a while and plan their next move.

The taxi vanished into the darkness and they headed inside to see what rooms they could get.

No rooms at all, it turned out. They were at a campsite. There were only a few tents still available—apparently some big equestrian event was taking place nearby in the morning. Once again, Steve paid up for two tents. It was agreed he would share with Matt and Carra, while Elena and Tima and Callie shared another.

The tents, at the furthest edge of the site, were basic—square and white with a single pole in the centre to lift the canvas up in a peak above their heads. Thick red and gold woven rugs were laid out across the sandy floor and low futon-style beds were positioned around the edges. A long coffee table, made of dark, carved wood, sat in the centre of the rug with a lantern glowing on it. The toilets were in portable units a short walk away.

They bought some water and some spiced chicken curry and flatbreads from the shop and café, which appeared to be open around the clock for guest campers. Then they sat together in one of the tents, eating quietly. It was warm inside and they all shook off their outer clothing as they ate and drank.

'It is simple,' said Carra, when they finally began to talk. 'I must go back to the tower tonight and climb it again. This time I will climb the whole thing from the outside and reach the top without arrest.'

'Carra—that's crazy!' said Callie. 'It's far too dangerous. You'll be up there for *hours*. That's if you can even *get* as far as the tower. The whole area could be under water!'

'It's not,' said Elena, consulting a world news site on her

phone. 'The water has receded.' She gulped and looked up at them all. 'But it's worse back home. Much worse.' She turned the phone around to show them the headline: **BREAKING NEWS **** EAST COAST OF ENGLAND SUBMERGED IN FREAK TIDAL SURGE.**

Steve groaned and rubbed his face. 'This is what I was dreading. If *this* area had a surge, with its shallow seas, other parts of the planet would have to be getting it much worse.'

'How bad is it?' murmured Callie, looking sick. 'Is Thornleigh swept away?'

'No . . . the sea has only flooded low-lying coastal areas,' said Elena. 'No reports of deaths yet.'

'There will be,' said her mother, grimly. 'I remember my gran talking about the tidal surge of 1953. Hundreds of people died in that one. And this is probably worse.'

'It's nothing,' said Steve, 'compared to what's to come. If we don't find a way to stop it.'

'It's already really scary,' said Elena, spooling down the small screen. The headlines were genuinely terrifying:

FLOODWATERS ENGULF COASTLINES AROUND EUROPE

FREAK WILDFIRES RAGE ACROSS MEXICO, CALIFORNIA, AND TEXAS

EARTHQUAKES SHAKE ITALY, SPAIN, AND NORTH AFRICA

TSUNAMI WARNINGS ACROSS THE PACIFIC

WORLD LEADERS PLAN EMERGENCY SUMMIT

'And we've not even reached three seconds,' murmured Matt.

Tima felt her stomach churn and wondered whether eating that curry was wise. She might be about to lose it all through sheer panic.

'So,' said Carra, reaching behind Elena for her bag and jacket. 'I must go back to the city. Now. There is no time to lose.'

'Carra—you have to rest! You're exhausted,' said Elena, trying to wrestle her bag and jacket away from her.

'You have seen the headlines,' stated Carra. 'With every hour that passes, the danger grows. The storm has barely begun.'

'A few more hours won't make that much difference,' said Callie. 'Come on, love. You need to rest.'

'There is no time,' insisted Carra. 'This is why you called me here. I have travelled from another galaxy! I must fix this problem.'

'Without us?' said Matt. 'I thought you said you needed us all there. *We* can't climb up the tower, even if you can.'

'Ideally, yes, you would all come with me,' said Carra. 'But it seems this cannot happen, so I must try alone.'

Suddenly Elena put an arm around Carra and spoke to her gently. 'You'll never be able to climb the tower with no rest. It will take you *hours* and you're so tired.' She took a deep breath and patted the surprised alien woman's cheek with her cupped palm. 'You *must* get some sleep first,' she said, in a rather

155

strangled voice.

'There is no time to sleep,' said Carra. And then she fell asleep.

'Don't breathe, everyone,' croaked Elena. As Carra slumped sideways onto the futon Elena held up the small shiny pouch that she'd fished out of the sleeve of Carra's green leather jacket. 'I've just knocked her out with her own sleep vapour. Let's get outside before it knocks us out too.'

Startled, everyone covered their noses and mouths and scrambled out of the tent where they stood, taking lungfuls of air and glancing back at Carra as she slumbered deeply on the futon.

'Had to do it,' puffed Elena, getting her breath back. 'Nothing was going to stop her. I think it should last a couple of hours—and that might be enough.'

'Well,' said Callie. 'That was . . . surprising.'

'She's a surprising girl,' said Matt. 'She sent an underworld god to sleep once . . .'

'Another time,' said Elena, as Callie and Steve stared at her.

'Yes,' said Callie. 'We all need some sleep—it's way past midnight. We can get up at dawn and work out what to do next.'

'Lucky,' said Matt, as he and Steve went back into the tent with Carra, who was very slightly snoring, 'I need you to be on alert. If Carra moves, you have to wake me up.'

Elena handed him the shiny pouch of sleep vapour. 'Don't squeeze it again unless you have to. Only if she wakes up in the next hour or so. She's got to get a couple of hours at least.'

But Carra slept on through the dark hours and so, after a

short while, did everyone else. Until 4.34 a.m. precisely when Tima sat up, just as if the beam had come through. Back home it *was* coming through and she couldn't possibly feel it . . . and yet. Elena was up too, staring across at her. 'It's time,' she said.

Outside they found Matt stepping out into the pre-dawn light, Lucky on his shoulder. It felt almost normal, just the three of them, standing together in the dark again, while everyone around them slept.

'We need to be somewhere,' said Tima. She held out her palm and Elena and Matt gasped. A scorpion sat in it, its claws raised and its sting arched over its body.

'I know,' said Matt and Elena, in unison.

They stepped away from the tents and climbed up a dune. The air around them was cool but there was still warmth radiating up from the ground. The moon, lower in the sky as dawn approached, cast silvery light across the desert, picking out the undulating landscape in crisp monochrome. It was spectacularly beautiful, its sands rippling like a dry sea. There was movement everywhere. It wasn't just sand. It was hundreds . . . *thousands* . . . of scorpions. Shiny carapaces glinting in the moonlight, they were travelling east.

There was no doubt about it. The Night Speakers were meant to follow.

CHAPTER 25

Matt had no idea where the camels had come from. As they crested yet another dune, three leggy creatures were padding across the sand towards them, already saddled up. They were roped together and the leader had a tether dangling from its furry chin. No keeper was anywhere in sight.

Elena squeaked in delight and stumbled down the ever-shifting hillside to greet them. Matt and Tima watched as the creatures clustered around her and bumped their noses against her face. The camels had neatly avoided the convoy of scorpions still leading them to the east. They seemed totally unfazed by the mass of arachnids.

'Are we meant to ride them?' asked Matt, looking uneasy.

'I think so,' said Tima. 'Don't worry—it's easy. I did it yesterday.'

'With these guys?' asked Matt.

'No—I don't think we've met before,' said Tima.

'They've come to help!' said Elena, beaming up at them as they stepped and slid down towards her. 'They're going to take us there quicker!'

Elena took the lead camel, untying it from the others. Tima separated the second two. The camels knelt and Tima showed Matt and Elena how to get up onto the soft fabric saddles and hold on. Matt slung one leg over the creature's furry back, wondering how on earth he was going to manage this. It was all right for Tima—she was a posh kid who went horse riding. All he'd ever ridden was a bike.

'Whoaa!' He felt a surge of alarm as his mount stood up and began to lope quickly east, alongside the winding lane of scorpions. He gripped the handle on the saddle and tried to get used to the swaying motion, while Lucky fluttered above him, making affronted chirps.

'It's OK—you get used to it,' called Tima, who was up on her camel and trotting along behind him as if she'd been born to it. 'Just relax and find your balance.'

Elena too was riding with ease; of course her instinctive mammal connection would be helping. Matt reminded himself that *he* could talk to mammals too and sent his camel a request to slow down a little and let him get used to this alarming motion. The camel glanced back at him and *did* slow down for a while; enough for Lucky to land on his shoulder and hold on tightly as he bobbed and swayed.

A downdraft of night air made him look up; a shadowy

creature was in flight just above his head. An *owl?*

'Look!' he called to the others. 'We've got more company.'

'Oh!' cried Tima. 'He's so beautiful!'

It was hard to make out the detail but, as it coasted past his head repeatedly, flying in slow loops to stay close to the party on the ground, Matt was fairly sure it was a scops owl. Its tree bark camouflage feathers, its piercing round orange eyes, and its finely-tipped ear tufts were just like a scops. *Are you here to guide us, too?* he asked it, mentally.

Yes, it replied, directly to his mind.

Where are we going?

Help, it told him. *Help.*

'What are your guys telling you?' Matt asked Tima and Elena.

'They're taking us to someone who can help, I think,' said Elena. She sounded happy. So did Tima when she agreed. Matt understood. They were all completely connected. The wildlife around them had seamlessly linked with their minds. For the first time in the past two days, Matt felt a genuine flicker of hope.

As the sun came up, warming the sand and the air rapidly, their guard changed. The scorpions, nocturnal creatures, gradually sank away under the sand—apart from the one Tima carried, which she invited to nestle inside the hood of her zip-up top, away from the heat. The owl still coasted over Matt's head but, just after daybreak, it was joined by what Matt was fairly sure were three greater spotted eagles. Lucky stayed put on his shoulder; not scared but tired. He wanted her close, and she knew it.

After an hour of journeying over endless, rolling sand dunes, broken only by occasional rocky outcrops and small clusters of desert shrubs, they reached an oasis. It lay in a shallow valley— an oval of shimmering green, bordered by high date palms and some incongruously lush lawns. A straight, well-maintained road ran directly up to its gates.

Matt squinted through the soft light. 'Is that . . . a race course?'

'For horse racing,' agreed Elena. 'Looks amazing, doesn't it?'

The closer they got, the more the oasis revealed its opulence. Golden sandstone walls ran around the perimeter, topped with ornate gilded metalwork and a series of pillars with golden domed turrets. An ornamental lake sparkled under the early sun, a fountain playing at its centre. Several expensive cars were parked under white awnings.

Matt was intrigued to see more, but the camels had other ideas. They turned south, to pad along the ridge and steadily make their way to the southern end of the racecourse oasis, far from its grand entrance.

The camels carried them to the perimeter wall some distance from the entrance and then they stopped.

'What now?' asked Tima. 'There's no way in here!'

'Well . . . there kind of is,' said Elena, pointing to an acacia tree. It grew close to the golden wall and its branches stretched out above the delicate gilded metalwork.

'You mean we're breaking in?' said Matt. 'Again?' He sighed.

'Come on,' said Elena. 'Where's your sense of adventure?'

'We're on camels,' said Matt, stonily. 'Trekking through the Arabian Desert after escaping arrest in the tallest tower in the world, then drugging an alien and following a stampede of scorpions.'

'Well,' said Elena, 'when you put it like *that*.' She grinned at him as her camel rode directly under the branches of the tree. She reached up, grabbed a handhold, and then curled her legs up off the saddle and into the acacia. Matt sighed and allowed his mount to take him to the same place, getting in line behind Tima while the owl and the eagles flapped down to perch in the higher branches.

Two minutes later they were edging out over the wall and scanning the drop. Beneath them was a perfectly maintained lawn with a thick border of colourful flowers. It looked like a fairly soft landing. Elena went first, dangling down from the branch as far as she could before letting go. She hit the flower bed and rolled across the turf with a gentle '*Doof!*'

Then Tima followed, landing like a gymnast. Matt, ten seconds later, landed hard enough to grunt loudly. He got up fast, rubbing his bruised backside, and scanned their location. It was the business end of the racecourse. There were several horseboxes lined up in a gravelled parking area just beyond a fine screen of slender palm trees. Beyond the boxes was what looked like a training area—a circle of compacted sand surrounded by simple wooden fencing. In the training circle a beautiful dapple grey stallion was attended by three men dressed in Arabic clothing; long white shirts and flowing white headdresses held in place with black circlets. As the heat of the day was already getting up, Matt could understand the appeal of this gear. It would be cool and comfortable.

'OK . . . so now what?' he asked. Tima and Elena looked uncertain.

'We're meant to be here,' said Tima. 'I just don't know why.'

'We should keep back—stay hidden,' said Matt. 'If they find us we could get banged up in an Arabian prison, like Carra nearly did.'

'No,' said Elena. 'We're not here to hide.'

Matt blinked and then realized what she meant. They had been brought here to find help. The camels had very definitely deposited them right by the training ground. Whoever was going to help them was here—now. He glanced back and saw the three eagles and the owl sitting high in the tree, staring down at them all expectantly.

'Is it them?' he called, softly, pointing across to the men and the horse.

The birds flapped wings in unison and seemed to *nod*. Lucky, back on his shoulder, said: '*Them.*'

'OK,' he said to Elena. 'You're right. We need to go and introduce ourselves.'

He took a deep breath, pulled back his shoulders, and walked between the trees, past the nearest horsebox and across to the wooden fence. Tima and Elena followed him, also adopting a very confident walk.

Why not? he asked himself. If they didn't find help here it wasn't the end of the world.

Oh, no—scratch that. It was.

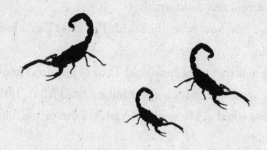

CHAPTER 26

Elena felt her skin prickle as the three of them walked up to the wooden fence and she rested her arms along the top of it. This was going to be one of those moments ... those moments when the world seemed to pause, hushed, awaiting what was destined to follow.

She became acutely aware of herself and her dearest friends, seeing them from an almost out of body perspective—Matt, tall, steady, and serious, with Lucky sitting on his shoulder; his jaw set and determined; no hint of the sullen bully-boy look he had worn for years before they became friends. Tima, moving like a dancer, her long dark hair in shining plaits and her brown eyes liquid and beautiful; so self-possessed and brave, stepping up onto a lower plank of wood to rest her arms along the top, a warm smile settling on her face as her scorpion friend nestled flat on her wrist like an exotic bracelet.

And then herself; fair hair blowing loose around her face; her blue eyes calm and resolved. Quiet. Waiting. Elena hoped whoever they met would see them for who they were.

Que sera, sera, as the old song went. *Whatever will be, will be.*

She fleetingly thought of Spin. Where was he now? Did he belong in this scene too? Fate hadn't allowed it, so she guessed not. Not this time.

The men by the horse eventually became aware of their audience. The one in the centre with an immaculately groomed beard and moustache suddenly turned his head towards them. His eyes—dark and intelligent—met Elena's and his eyebrows drew together in surprise and curiosity as he glanced from Elena to Matt to Tima. He seemed completely at ease—but the same could not be said of his two companions. Both men suddenly leapt in front of him and began to shout—in a mixture of Arabic and English.

'What are you doing here? This is a private area! What is the meaning of this? Who are you?'

'Say nothing,' breathed Elena. 'Be still. Wait.'

The two men were still blocking the other man protectively; clearly he was a man of some status. But as they continued to bark questions and as one of them retrieved a handgun from inside his robes and held it up, the first man called out: 'Stop! They are just children!' Then he pushed his way past his bodyguards and strode towards the fence.

Nearing them, he paused a few steps away, while the men followed close, one—probably the trainer—tightly holding the reins of the stallion, which was shifting nervously and jerking against its halter, the other still brandishing the gun and now pulling a two-way radio out of that well-stocked robe.

'Ssshhh—wait!' said the main man. 'Don't call anybody. We don't need a circus.'

He stepped a little closer. 'Who are you?' he said, in perfect English, his eyes coming to rest on Elena. 'Why are you in my grounds?'

Elena took a breath and said: 'I'm Elena, she's Tima, and he's Matt . . . and that . . .' she indicated the fourth member of their party on Matt's shoulder, '. . . is Lucky.'

Lucky obliging said: '*Lucky*,' making the man's eyes flicker across to her in intrigued amusement for a second.

'We don't exactly know why we're here,' went on Elena, realizing she had slipped into fluent Arabic as the man's eyes widened slightly in surprise—she looked very English after all. 'Some camels brought us . . . and a lot of scorpions . . .' Tima held up her wrist and her scorpion friend raised its tail in salute. '. . . and the owl and the eagles.' Elena pointed up over her shoulder and heard the eagles flap their wings and give a low yipping sound while the owl gave a creaky grunt.

'Sir—what is this?' growled the man with the gun, but the main man raised his hand abruptly and his guard fell silent.

'We think they brought us here,' Elena went on, 'because they believe you can help us. Help . . . the planet.'

'What do they think I can do for you, exactly?' asked the man, folding his hands together in front of him.

'Well . . . I don't know for sure,' went on Elena. 'But we came to this country to get to the top of the Burj Khalifa. Our friend needs to send a signal from the very top. Have you heard about the flooding in Dubai? The tidal surges here and around the world? Have you heard about the wildfires and the earthquakes . . . ?'

The man narrowed his eyes and nodded. 'I have heard.'

'We know what's causing them,' said Elena. 'And we think we know how to fix it—but we can't do it on our own.'

'Can you help?' asked Tima. 'Do you have friends at the Burj Khalifa? Could you ask them to let us go all the way up?'

The man's face twitched for a moment and then he laughed, shaking his head. 'You came all the way here—and broke into my training grounds—to ask for a free trip up a tourist attraction?'

'You don't understand,' said Matt, and at the sound of his voice, low and terse, the other men tensed again. Elena realized that Matt was no child in their eyes—he was fifteen; a tall young man with determination blazing in his eyes. He looked like a threat.

'Show them Lucky,' she said, quietly. 'Hold her up on both hands.' She did not want to give those men the slightest chance to believe Matt was dangerous.

'There is something on the dark side of the moon,' Elena went on, keeping her gaze steadily on the main man, while Matt held Lucky out with both hands steepled together for a steady perch. 'Something from another galaxy. It is slowing the planet down, second by second. This is why the tides are messed up. It's bad . . . and it's going to get worse. If we don't do something about it . . . this time next week . . .' she glanced around her, '. . . your beautiful racecourse could be under the sea.'

The man looked at her thoughtfully, tilting his head to one side as he considered her words. 'Forgive me . . . ah . . . Elena,' he said, now back in English. 'You seem quite serious, but you will have to admit that your story is very hard to believe.'

Elena nodded. 'I know. It sounds insane. But we flew all the way from England to save the world. We can't give up. If you come with us to our campsite you can meet an earth scientist who will back up what we're telling you . . . and my—my mum.' She winced a little. 'And Carra—our friend who is going to send a message from the top of the tower and get help from her people . . . if you can just help us to get her there. She tried to climb up it yesterday, but she got stopped—and nearly arrested.'

'Elena,' said the man, looking sorrowful. 'You are a very interesting young lady and so are your friends and their . . . pets. You tell me a fascinating story and I would like to know more but I am expecting important guests and I must prepare my horse for the race.'

'Your horse won't run,' said Tima.

The man raised an eyebrow at her. 'Really?' he said, while his men simply looked enraged, as if nobody ever spoke out of turn to their boss.

'No,' said Tima. 'Not if we tell him not to. There are more important things to do.'

'I have given you my time,' said the man. 'And I have not allowed my men to march you away at gunpoint, because I do not wish to be rude to any of my guests—even uninvited ones.

But I really must finish this talk and you must be guided back to the exit. Your parents called, perhaps.'

The stallion suddenly began blowing and grunting and pulling against its trainer. 'Whoa! Calm, my boy, calm!' he said, but the stallion pulled hard on its halter and then turned its head and walked back across the training area, dragging the trainer away in a cloud of sand. The main man looked baffled and called out to the horse but it just tossed its mane and walked on, despite the trainer's best attempts to anchor it to the spot.

The man turned back to them, staring in disbelief. 'What *is* this?'

'Shall I bring him back?' asked Elena. She sent a message: *Come to me*. The horse immediately turned and trotted directly over to her and rested its chin in her outstretched palm. The trainer, towed after it, gaped at her while the other two looked at each other and then back at the horse in amazement.

'Sing for me,' said Elena, aloud, for the benefit of her audience. The horse lifted its head and gave a long, high whinny. 'And again,' she said. The horse repeated the performance. 'And now kiss the one you love best,' she said. The horse swung its head around and nuzzled the main man directly in the face, making him splutter and push the creature away with firmness but evident fondness.

'She's some kind of horse whisperer,' said the trainer in a low, impressed voice.

'Not just horses,' said Elena. '*Come on then*'. Along the top of the fence ran a ripple of soft sandy fur. Desert rats were emerging from the flowerbeds and beneath the horse trailers, scaling the posts and walking the flat wooden planking. The men were clearly astonished—and positively staggered when Elena said: 'Stop!' and the gerbils all paused, whiskers trembling. 'Sit up, please,' she added, and they all sat up, front paws raised.

'What is *this?*' murmured the bodyguard, eyes wide. 'What trickery?'

'Better go now,' said Elena, and the desert rats departed. 'Matt—you next.'

Matt raised both his hands and Lucky rose up in the air, to be met by the owl and the eagles, and then . . . within a matter of seconds . . . a whole host of birds, emerging from the carefully-planted oasis trees and flying in a circle just a couple of metres above their heads, fluttering the head cloths of the astonished men with their downdraft.

'Malvoleo!' cried the main man, spinning around and staring up, flabbergasted. Elena realized a falcon with jesses on its feet had joined the flock.

'Now you, Tima,' said Elena.

Tima smiled and deposited her scorpion friend on the fence. 'Over here!' she called, because everyone's eyes were still on the birds. 'Terry! Please walk left . . .' The scorpion strolled to her left. 'And right . . .' And to her right. 'Sting up.' It raised its sting. 'Sting down.' It lowered it.

The men looked dazed. The trainer had dropped the horse's reins and the bodyguard's gun dangled in one hand. The main man was staring at the dancing scorpion as if he was in a dream.

'Settle down, everyone,' said Elena. At once the wildlife departed, the horse came and rested its head on her shoulder and the trained falcon landed on Matt's outstretched arm and nudged lovingly at his nose with its curved yellow beak.

'Do we have your attention now?' asked Elena, softly, as she stroked the stallion's soft mane.

'Bahar,' said the man. 'Cancel everything.'

'Sir . . . ?'

'*Everything*. We need to take these young people to the Burj.'

CHAPTER 27

'She drugged me!' Carra looked absolutely furious.

'Sssshhh now,' said Callie. 'Have some breakfast!' She put a platter of fruit, yoghurt, dates, and nuts in front of the angry alien.

'It was a pretty smooth move,' said Steve. 'You have to admit it.'

Carra had woken up coughing after a straight seven hours of sleep and was aghast to find herself left behind with the grown-ups while the Night Speakers had gone off into the desert.

'Why did you let them go? Why didn't you wake me?' Carra demanded, picking up a date and stuffing it in her mouth.

'We didn't know they'd gone,' said Callie. 'We only woke up ourselves an hour ago. They must all have slipped away in the night.'

'Where? Where did they go?' Carra shoved in a chunk of pineapple and chewed on it as if it had personally angered her.

'We don't know,' said Steve. 'All we've had is a text from Elena, saying don't worry and they're on their way back with help. They should be here any time now.'

Carra put down her plate and fixed him with such a stare that he quailed inside. 'You, of all people,' she said, 'should understand that time is not on our side.'

'I, of all people,' he replied, 'entirely understand. The world is beginning to unravel. Panic is spreading across social media. The Ring of Fire—that's a circle of undersea volcanoes in the Pacific—is just beginning to kick off with some unprecedented eruptions, which will almost certainly lead to catastrophic tsunamis. This time yesterday I was meant to be briefing the Prime Minister of Great Britain and warning of all of this—but instead I committed career suicide and hopped on a plane to Dubai. And look, here I am in the middle of a bloody desert, waiting for three kids and a starling to come back and tell me what to do!'

Carra dropped her stare and ate a spoonful of yoghurt.

'It's pretty freaky, isn't it?' said Callie. 'I've always lived in dread of big catastrophes. I have bipolar disorder and when I'm in my lows, I can hardly breathe for fear of what might happen to Elena, or me, or anyone I know, out in the big wide world. But now that something catastrophic *is* happening . . . I'm weirdly calm.' She put her hand on his arm. 'Thank you,' she said. 'God knows how this is going to end but I will never forget what you have done, putting your whole career on the line to come here with us. Paying for everything . . . *believing* my daughter.' And she kissed him on the cheek. Which was not unpleasant.

'And you,' said Callie, turning back to Carra. 'Stop making such a fuss and wait. Elena knows what she's doing. If she says she's bringing help, she's bringing help! And whether it's the whole Emirate army or half a dozen bats, I don't care. She's bringing help.'

'Hi.' They spun around to see Elena standing under the awning. 'We've brought someone who can get you up the tower, Carra.' She stood aside to allow an Arabian man, dressed in white, to enter the tent. Matt and Tima were close behind, suppressing grins.

'Mum, Steve . . . Carra . . .' said Elena. 'I'd like you to meet Sheikh Akeem bin Rashid Al-Hashim.'

An elegantly-attired man held out a hand to Steve and said: 'Please . . . call me Hazza.'

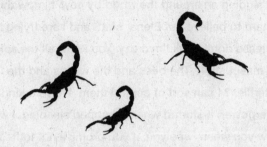

CHAPTER 28

Getting back into Dubai was a great deal easier than leaving it. The sheikh—who had now insisted that *everyone* call him Hazza—had a large people carrier built for travelling the desert with his retinue. Followed by his security team in another 4x4, he drove the vehicle himself while sharing rapid conversation with Steve.

The Night Speakers listened and didn't say much. Tima felt waves of exhaustion rolling over her and realized just how little sleep she'd had in the past two days. She watched as Elena's head slowly sank onto her mother's shoulder, eyes closing, and felt a huge pang of guilt and sadness. Without reading any texts that had been left for her—she could not bear the pain of it—she composed another message to Mum's phone.

Mum and Dad. You must know about all the crazy stuff that's going on around the world by now. I know this will be hard to believe but Elena, Matt, and I are trying to stop it. Please don't think I'm crazy. You know all the spider and insect stuff? The bees and the wasps and the butterflies? I can sort of control them. I have a kind of superpower; it started when I stopped sleeping. I will show you when I see you, if you promise not to freak out. I'm telling you this now because . . .

She paused. Why *was* she telling Mum and Dad this now? Of all the times she had imagined revealing her secret, she'd never pictured doing it by text while riding through the desert in a big Jeep with an actual, real life sheikh at the wheel. Truth was, she didn't know how much time any of them had left. If Carra couldn't send her message and get her people to create a solar flare to blast that Ayotian ship off the dark side of the moon, everybody's days were seriously numbered. Mum and Dad might just as well know everything.

. . . I'm telling you this now because I've kept it from you for too long. Elena and Matt have special powers too. Elena is good with mammals and Matt with birds. Elena has told her mum but Matt's parents don't know. Also, we have an alien friend who is going to try to stop the world slowing down and falling apart. We have to help her. Wish us luck.

I love you. xxx

As she pressed SEND she became aware of Matt watching her. He gave her a tight, sad smile, obviously working out who she'd been texting. Tima smiled sadly back at him. 'Matt . . . do you want to text *your* mum?'

Matt nodded. 'Thanks,' he said, taking her mobile. She didn't see what he texted but she could guess; probably something similar to hers. Definitely ending in *I love you.*

'We can do this,' she said, glancing at Carra who was watching the desert slide past and the glittering city emerge on the horizon in the morning sun. She had not spoken since they'd all got back. She looked serious; focused.

The conversation in the front slowed and stopped and suddenly the sheikh pulled the car over to the side of the road and killed the engine. He paused for a moment, looking ahead through the windscreen, and then he turned around and addressed Carra.

'I am told you are not from this planet,' he said, in English.

Carra looked at him and did not reply.

'May I know which planet you *are* from?' he persisted.

'Targa,' she said. 'It is beyond your galaxy.'

'Then I thank you for coming to our aid,' he said. 'I am finding it hard to believe you really are an . . . alien . . . yet my new scientist friend here is convinced of it, and after the most extraordinary feats I have seen Elena, Matt, and Tima perform this morning, I am preprared to believe a great deal more than I might have yesterday.'

It occurred to Tima that he was speaking just like a royal addressing a world leader . . . which, in a way, he was. Carra was the only representative of Targa here on Earth. Tima liked the way his words were filled with respect; she and Matt and Elena should probably speak to Carra that way. Carra *was* something awe-inspiring.

'Do you think you can restore the planet to its normal rotation?' Hazza went on.

'It is possible,' she said. 'But I cannot guarantee it. I must send my message, and to do that I must be high up in a static location. I had hoped for a kilometre from the surface. This will be just 828 metres. I hope it is enough.'

'And your people—if they get the message—what will they do?'

'They will enable me to create a solar flare,' said Carra. 'A directional flare of plasma from your sun which will wipe out the threat hiding behind your moon.'

'That is something I hope to see,' said Hazza. He turned back and re-started the engine. 'I've had the tower cleared,' he said. 'Nobody will stand in your way.'

He wasn't joking. When they arrived, three men and two women—all impeccably dressed—were waiting for them outside a private entrance that only the sheikh's cars had access to.

'Your Royal Highness,' said the most senior of the men, with a slight bow. 'We are delighted to assist you today.' His eyes fell upon Carra, clearly recognizing her, and his expression flickered. 'You are entirely happy about this, er, expedition, sir?'

'I am, thank you,' said Hazza. 'My friends need full access to the top. I will be accompanying them.'

'And . . . your security detail too, I trust,' said the senior manager, looking only slightly troubled while, Tima guessed, wild klaxons of alarm were probably going off behind that professional smile.

Hazza rested his hand on the manager's shoulder. 'Ahmed, I know this all seems very worrying,' he said. 'But please trust me. I believe these people can help us with some much bigger problems than my security.'

The manager visibly relaxed. 'Well, Your Highness, if you are happy, I am happy. Please—everyone—come this way.'

The lift took them all up again at breathtaking speed, but at least this time they all had a plan. A *real* plan. What would they have done if their animal friends hadn't taken them to find Hazza? Tima wondered. It would never have occurred to any of them simply to ask for help like this. No—they would have come back with Carra and watched, terrified, as she insisted on climbing up the outside.

At the 154th floor they had to get out. The rest of the tower was not served by an elevator; they'd need to climb the stairs. The lobby here had an even more spectacular view than the 148th floor. From this height they could just about see the tiny dots of emergency vehicles running some kind of clean-up after yesterday's tidal surge. The damage caused was hard to make out from this distance but during the Jeep ride, their phones getting a much needed charge from sockets by their seats, Elena had shown them all images of cars being carried away by seawater. Seven deaths had so far been reported.

'I think,' said Hazza, turning to Steve and Callie, 'this may be a good place for you to wait.'

Steve and Callie stared at him, at each other, and then at everyone else. 'We need to stay here?' checked Callie, instinctively reaching out and stroking Elena's hair.

'Yes. It is comfortable.' Hazza indicated a long leather sofa arranged by the glass wall. 'You have a good view. I hope you won't need to wait too long. But the climb from here on in only gets more difficult, and space, in the spire, is very limited. At that point it will be only two or three of us—and the abseil manager. Do you understand?'

'The abseil manager?' squeaked Callie, her eyes round.

'An abseiling team keeps the tower clean all year round,' he explained. 'The manager knows how to harness everyone up and keep them safe.'

'Good . . . good,' breathed Callie. 'Harnesses sound good.'

Steve put an arm around her. 'They'll be fine,' he said.

Elena added: 'Of *course* we'll be fine. We'll be back in no time. Probably won't even get up to the top, anyway—that'll be Carra.'

'Do you even *need* to go on up, then?' asked Callie. 'I mean . . . surely only Carra actually has to go up now?'

'I will require them,' said Carra. She didn't explain why and, not for the first time since knowing her, Tima felt a chill. Carra could be coldly efficient when it came to carrying out what she saw as her duty. A few months ago she'd been quite prepared to incinerate half the UK in order to save the rest of the world from deadly alien seeds.

'We'll be fine—and I'm not missing this for the world!' Tima said, almost managing to sound genuinely excited.

When they'd gone, Steve led Callie to the sofa and they sat down to gaze out at the stunning panorama. From here they could see the curve of the earth. The marble-tiled lobby ran two thirds of the way around the building, offering views at every angle, out west across the sea, down to the sparkling oasis of the great city and east, into the desert.

'Well, if the end of the world *is* coming,' said Callie, taking his hand, 'at least we've got the best view.'

Steve squeezed her fingers, nodding, and then narrowed his eyes. 'What's that?' he said.

'What?'

'That . . . on the horizon.'

Callie stood up and stared.

Then she said: 'Oh no.'

CHAPTER 29

It was nearly 6.40 a.m. and well past Spin's bedtime. But even if he'd tried he would not have been able to sleep through the deafening drumming. And the fear.

'What the hell is going on out there?' said Astrid, standing at the window and staring at the garden. What little of it she could see was being pounded by the most violent deluge the town of Thornleigh had ever seen. She'd planted many EPP-friendly shrubs and trees over the years. Some were there purely to give plenty of shade. Others were planted to be appreciated after sunset—attractive leafy plants which glistened by moonlight, and flowers, like night-scented stock and evening primrose, which let out their sweet scent purely after dark, for the moths and bats. And porphyriacs.

Most of these were now flattened.

Spin switched on the radio, tuned to the local BBC station.

'. . .to stay in. That's the advice from the emergency services,' said the presenter, sounding quite shaken. 'Please stay indoors. As well as the danger of flooding, the hail has been phenomenally large—and actually heavy enough to cause injury. Hospitals across East Anglia have admitted scores of people with severe bruising and even suspected concussion—and that's on top of all the casualties from yesterday's coastal surge.'

Astrid turned the panicky narration down and faced Spin. 'I don't know what's going on,' she said. 'But I think we need to be ready to travel. In case things get really bad. I'm thinking about *The Nightjar*. The roads might get jammed, but we can travel by canal boat fairly safely, I think. When this eases off I'm going to get some supplies into it. Just in case.'

Spin wondered, for the thirtieth or fortieth time, whether he should tell her what he knew. Since the departure of the Night Speakers with their crazy plan to take Carra to the highest manmade point on earth, he'd been scanning the news and watching everything steadily unravel. The floods on the coast were the point when the media truly started waking up, especially when everyone realized freak tidal surges were happening all around the globe. Then the earthquakes . . . the wildfires . . . the undersea volcanoes. All of it fitted with what that scientist had said.

'Mum,' said Spin, surprising her, because he usually called her Astrid. 'I know why this is happening.'

'You do?' she raised an eyebrow, unconvinced.

'The rotation of the Earth is slowing down,' he said. 'It's

slowed down by just over two seconds over the past three or four days. And it's going to keep slowing down. In a full week it will have slowed down by three seconds. That's why the tides have gone insane . . . and now the weather.'

Astrid studied his face. 'Are you serious?'

Spin opened the laptop on the kitchen island and showed her the assorted science sites he'd found where this theory had been gaining momentum.

'Well . . . that's just conjecture,' said Astrid. 'It doesn't mean—'

'It's true,' said Spin.

'But . . . why aren't we being told?'

'Because of the panic,' said Spin. The powers that be *must* have discovered the truth by now; Dr Baxendale had been due to brief the PM yesterday morning—but there had been no official press call and Spin wasn't a bit surprised. He was very panicked himself; only just hanging on to his composure, in fact. Imagine multiplying *that* by more than 50 million.

Astrid sat down on a kitchen stool with a bump, staring at her feet. 'Well . . . that's it then. It's all over . . . wow.'

'It's not necessarily all over,' said Spin. 'I have these . . . *friends*, I suppose you would call them.'

'Friends?' echoed Astrid. 'Really? You mean . . . that girl?' She smiled thinly. 'You really liked her, didn't you?'

'Hell's teeth, Mother!' burst out Spin. 'The end of the world is nigh and you're still hoping I might get a girlfriend?!'

'Whatever!' Astrid flapped her hands. 'Get to the point!'

'Right,' said Spin, taking a moment. He had no idea where

Elena was right now but he'd just seen her face flicker through his mind, and found himself wishing, really wishing, that he might see the real thing again before everything fell apart. He shook his head. *Seriously. Get a grip.* 'These friends,' he went on, 'well, we don't always get along, exactly.'

'You don't say?' said Astrid, drily.

'*But* . . . over the past few months we've had to work together to, well, save people. A lot of people.'

'O . . . kay,' said Astrid.

'Remember the power plant fire and the swarms of wasps? That was one of our fun nights out,' said Spin. 'Then the time when the whole town couldn't breathe? Another one. And the weird thing with the reservoir and the dead doctors and the brainwashed kids . . . ?'

'When you came back pretty brainwashed yourself for a few weeks?' said Astrid, looking suddenly enlightened.

'Yes, that,' said Spin. 'Well—stick with me here—*aliens* had a part in it. There's a weird connection between Thornleigh and aliens. They pop in from time to time. But not all of them are intent on world domination; one of them is friendly and she *might* just help us save the day.'

'Sure,' said Astrid, rubbing her face. 'Why not?'

Spin sighed and then opened his mouth to go on but at that point the rain abruptly stopped and he could hear an odd clicking, scraping noise. Narrowing his eyes he pulled back the long curtain that hung across the door to the back garden. Outside, looking bedraggled but determined, sat a fox.

'What the hell . . . ?' murmured Astrid.

'Oh yes,' said Spin, opening the door to allow the soggy creature inside. 'And I forgot to mention, these, um, friends of mine—they can all speak to animals. This is Elena's fox buddy, Velma. She doesn't much like me, but she's helped me out once or twice. What is it, Velma?'

The vixen shook vigorously, like a dog, scattering raindrops in all directions and then stared intently into his eyes before turning around and stepping back into the garden, her tail high and twitchy. You didn't need to have Night Speaking superpowers to work out that she badly wanted him to follow.

Spin stood in the doorway. The dark grey clouds had lifted, almost as suddenly as they'd dropped, an hour ago. Rainwater was streaming off the leaves and roofs and pathways. Shafts of sun were already lighting the garden and an intensely bright rainbow was painting itself across the western sky.

'I can't go out in that,' said Spin. 'It's too bright.'

Velma stood and stared at him. Then she did something which made every hair on his body stand on end. She opened her jaws and her throat and she let out a blood-chilling scream.

'Jeeeeez!' called out Astrid.

There was a moment of silence and then the vixen did it again.

'I CAN'T!' yelled Spin when she'd stopped. 'I'm not one of your gang!'

Velma stared at him for a moment and then opened her jaws and screamed a third time, possibly even louder.

'She *really* wants your attention,' said his mother. She put a large black golfing umbrella in his hand.

'Seriously?' said Spin, holding it up, furled, like a sword.

'Maybe it's important,' said Astrid. 'Just stay covered up. The cloud is probably going to close over again soon.'

Spin cursed and flicked the umbrella open. He *never* used umbrellas. *Ever.* But the sun was already making his skin prickle and he had no idea where Velma wanted to take him. Also . . . those hailstones.

'All right!' he hissed, pulling his cowl hood up over his head and tugging the thin black sleeves of his silk coat down below his knuckles.

'Be careful, Spin,' called his mother as he followed the fox through the swamped back garden and out through the gate into the woods.

The trees kept grabbing at the umbrella so he snapped it shut all the while he was protected by the canopy of new spring leaves. Chinks of sunlight still danced across his path, though. He pulled dark sunglasses out of a pocket and put them on. 'This had better be good, you fur bag,' he muttered.

It was nearly half past seven by the time they reached the suburbs of Thornleigh. The roads were awash with rainwater and piles of white slush carpeted the grass verges where the massive hailstones had melted. All around him were conservatories and greenhouses with smashed roofs. Quite a lot of cracked glass in house windows too. His home would probably look the same if he and Astrid hadn't fitted wooden shutters to the outside of all the windows some time ago. Plenty of parked vehicles had shattered windscreens. The roads were eerily quiet now with only the occasional car or van struggling through, the drivers tense and watchful.

On a normal day most of the town would be squabbling over who was first in the shower, getting dressed, making toast, and pouring coffee. This morning Spin could *feel* the difference. Most of the people of Thornleigh would have been up since shortly after 5 a.m. when the freak weather had struck; nobody could have slept on through it. Some might now be going back to bed, giving up on travelling to work or school after listening to the radio. The schools would probably stay closed for the day in any case; there would be smashed glass everywhere. There was plenty of it just walking along the road towards the lower end of town.

They made an odd sight on an even odder day; the boy with the black umbrella and dark glasses and the red fox, picking their way carefully but swiftly through glass and melting ice and gushing streams of rainwater runoff.

'Um . . . do you *know* where we're going?' asked Spin, as the fox paused at a T-junction. *Right* led up into the main town, past RichToffsVille where Tima lived, and on to Elena's road and eventually up to the tower blocks and the estate and Kowski Kar Klean.

Left led to the power station and the Quarry End industrial estate and, down past it, some rundown terraces. These pebbledashed homes stood in the shadow of a high chalk cliff face, hewn out of the old hill by nineteenth-century quarry workers.

'Oh not Quarry End *again*,' groaned Spin as Velma set off left. 'Don't tell me there's more trouble brewing in the underworld.'

But Velma did not take him into Quarry End. Instead she skirted the length of its metal perimeter and then took a right turn into Quarry Terrace, keeping low as she ran along a line of parked cars. A few people were now emerging from their homes, staring, wide-eyed, at the state of their windscreens and their street. They barely noticed the fox and the tall Gothic-looking boy with a black umbrella.

Velma led him to the end of the street—a dead end. The almost sheer cliff face was mostly chalk and dotted with straggly buddleia plants. Velma stopped at the foot of it and looked up. She looked at Spin and then she looked up again, before circling agitatedly on the spot, her tail flicking.

'Well?' snapped Spin. 'Now what? What do you want me to do?'

Velma stared up at him with great intensity. Then she leapt up and put her front paws against the bramble-strewn foot of the cliff and made a yelping sound.

'You want me to *climb* that? Are you *insane?*'

A low rumble of thunder and a flurry of rain against the umbrella made him shiver. Velma dropped back to the ground and fixed him with an unwavering stare.

'Look,' said Spin. 'You seem to be mistaking me for one of your Night Speaker friends. I don't speak fox. And if I did and you really were suggesting I climb this—*gah! Stop it!*'

For Velma was screaming again. And then running away from the cliff. And then running back to it. She was deeply, deeply unhappy about the situation—that was obvious. She was out here in full daylight, with people around who could *see* her. In this, Spin definitely felt some sympathy for her.

'Right,' he said, folding down the umbrella and wincing in the light—which was thankfully getting dimmer as more rain clouds rolled in. 'I am going to go up just a little way, to prove to you that it's *just not possible*.'

But it *was* possible. It wasn't *sensible*, but for someone with Spin's agility and climbing skills, it was entirely possible. Once he'd found his hand and foot holds and begun to climb, it came to him very naturally. He was five or six metres up without even thinking. And then, as his hands and feet connected with the cold, damp cliff face, he began to sense something odd. Something *really* odd.

There was *movement*. He could sense it through his fingers. The cliff face was . . .

Spin caught his breath as he noticed the small chunks of chalk and pebble showering out of cracks. Cracks that looked fresh. Cracks that were spreading. Spin bellowed a long, single-syllable, heartfelt curse as he began to slide back down the undulating weedy outcrops.

Then, to the people down below, he screamed: 'RUN! RUUUN! THE CLIFF IS GOING TO FALL!'

Icy rain began to pound his head and shoulders as he descended, scrabbling to find the holds that had helped him up the cliff face. He screamed at the people again but now the hail was back and his voice was drowned out by the thundering of ice striking the road and roofs and cars. They were all running back inside their homes, obeying their common sense.

But they didn't know what was coming. Spin fell the last three metres, landing in a patch of brambles with a tremendous thwack which sent a bolt of pain through his shoulder. The pain took away his ability to inhale and for a few seconds all he knew was the sudden fire in his shoulder and the balls of ice punching his face.

But if there was one thing Spin was on first name terms with, it was pain. His shoulder was very possibly broken, but that wasn't going to stop him. Above him he could see more sliding chalk. The cliff face was absolutely sodden with rain and the whole hillside had clearly soaked up all it could take. The sheer weight of that much water was disintegrating it.

The people living in this street . . . and anyone working in Quarry End's warehouses and offices . . . they were going to be buried alive.

If he didn't get up.

With a whine of agony, Spin staggered to his feet, grabbed the umbrella, and ran to the nearest house, the storm of hail rebounding off him and making his boots slither on the pavement. He bashed on the door with his good arm until a man threw it open and glared at him.

'The cliff,' gasped Spin, fighting off waves of sickening pain down his right arm. 'It's going to fall. Get out! Get out NOW!'

CHAPTER 30

It was quite possible to imagine they were *not* nearly a kilometre off the surface of the planet. From where he was now, Matt could almost convince himself he was underground . . . in a shiny new sewer system or something.

They were climbing what felt like an endless run of metal staircases, zigzagging back and forth in a tight concrete and metal well.

Lucky wanted to fly up ahead of them but Matt told her firmly that she must stay where she was, awkwardly gripping the top of his hardhat with her delicate claws.

The sheikh and the alien (which sounded a bit like a West End musical, Matt thought, randomly) were climbing above him. Everyone but Carra had changed into blue boiler suits down on one of the access level floors—even Tima, who'd had to roll up the legs and arms of hers. Hazza's abseiling guy had also made them put on harnesses which could be clipped to safety rails inside the spire as they climbed. Then he'd reluctantly agreed to wait at the lower level, despite his very sincere concern. Nobody, it seemed, argued with Hazza.

Carra had refused to change out of her leather gear or put on a hat, despite everyone's best efforts to persuade her, but she consented to the harness. Her backpack was still firmly strapped over her shoulders and Matt was fervently hoping that everything she needed was in it. Now would not be a good time to discover she'd left something vital on another planet.

Matt glanced down and saw Elena and Tima close behind on the steep steps. 'Keep moving, slowpoke!' said Tima, headbutting him in the backside. He tried to laugh but couldn't. Fear was flinging itself around inside him like a trapped rat. Not just because they were about to step outside on the very tip of the tallest manmade structure on Earth—but because of what he could hear.

And feel.

The tower was being swept by massive gusts of wind. The metal groaned and clanked as a storm swirled around it.

'Don't worry,' called Hazza. 'It is normal—the tower is designed to manage the wind. It is quite safe.'

'But what about *that*?' asked Elena.

That was a singing, stinging, zinging noise.

Hazza did not reply for a while. He moved up close behind Carra and overtook her. 'Wait,' he said. 'Let me go ahead.'

The very last floor was the size of a small room—half of it

exposed on an open platform. The view would have been out of this world . . . if you could see it. As they emerged, puffing, sweating, and shaking with fatigue from the climb, they discovered the source of the singing, stinging, zinging sound.

Sand.

Hazza had taken off his hardhat and was resting his forehead against the glass of the doors to the platform. Outside the sky was as dark as dusk. 'We will have to wait,' he said. 'It will pass quickly.'

'I cannot wait,' said Carra, reaching for the door.

'You *must*,' insisted Hazza, gripping the handle. Then he suddenly grabbed her hand and held it up. Clutched in her palm was a small silver canister. 'How many times did you need this, just climbing this far?' he asked. 'Three, I counted. You are not breathing well even in here—imagine how you'll cope out there!'

Carra snatched her hand—and the inhaler—away and thrust the canister into her pocket. 'The gas mix on your planet is very similar to Targa,' she said. 'Just . . . not similar enough. I can survive here for a week, perhaps, with help from my inhaler. But I may not *get* a week if you hold me back much longer.'

There was a gleam of sunshine and then, with an eerie suddenness, the sandstorm had blown past them.

'Your wish is my command!' said Hazza, stepping aside and opening the door.

Carra stepped out onto the platform. It was crowded with aerials, satellite dishes, and huge uptilted lights with lenses the size of dustbin lids. Matt and the others followed her out, gaping at the view. It had been stunning down on level 160.

Here it was simply staggering. The curve of the Earth was clearly visible through the haze. Tima ran to the shoulder-height glass panels that guarded the edge, squeaking with wonder. Matt held Lucky tightly on his shoulder, afraid that the buffeting wind might spin her away. Elena leaned back against the door, taking long, slow breaths.

'Didn't know you had vertigo,' said Matt.

'Nor did I,' she breathed. 'Until now.'

They stared up at the final climb. Two hundred metres of steel stretched above them—a skinny metal finger poking into the heavens.

Carra had found another door in a curved wall of louvred metal. This was the access point to the final climb. They all followed her in. It was a tight squeeze. They were now inside the spire. Two iron ladders were set into the well of metal, rungs rising vertically on either side. Hazza saw to it that everyone was clipped firmly onto the rope ratchet system that ran from top to bottom of the rungs. 'If you need to rest, it will hold you safe,' he said. 'Put on the gloves—you will need the grip. It is a very long climb. You *will* need to rest.'

He wasn't wrong. Matt considered himself very fit, but climbing vertically was exhausting. Glancing up past the silhouettes of Carra and the sheikh he could make out light, shining through a distant grid. The topside of this was the final point at which a human being could stand on the tower.

When Carra reached it she climbed right up through. Matt expected Hazza to follow, but he did not. Instead he waited on the ladder as Matt—shaking with the effort of the climb and dripping with sweat—came up alongside him. Matt was very glad of the grip the gloves gave him. Hazza himself looked remarkably fresh. He'd done this before, of course.

'There is very little room,' said Hazza. 'And I think our alien friend would prefer one of *you* to keep her company.'

Matt gulped. 'Who do you want, Carra?'

Carra bent over to look down at them. 'I want all three of you,' she said.

'No,' said Hazza. 'You cannot all fit. Two people at the most.'

'Just take me,' said Matt. 'I can—'

'Do you understand the principle of power circuits?' cut in Carra.

Matt blinked. A physics lesson? *Now?*

'My communication device,' said Carra. 'It has a powerful reach. From 900 metres above sea level it can travel through a pan-dimensional web of connections and reach my people in five Earth minutes.'

'But . . . we're only 828 metres up!' called up Tima. 'Is that too short?'

'I don't know,' said Carra. 'It may be enough. It may not. For the best chance I need a boost. I need all of you to be connected to me to create a circuit.'

'We could all hold on to each other down here,' called up Elena. 'Tima can hold Matt's ankles and I can hold Tima and Matt can—'

'A *circuit!*' snapped Carra. 'A *ring* of power. Have you never made your own circuit while testing a battery? You send your electrical field in through both ends of the battery as you hold it in both hands . . . you close the circuit!'

'Oh,' said Elena. 'I see.'

Matt shook his head. 'How can we do that? How can we make a circuit if we can't all fit up there?'

The metal floor Carra now stood on was just a circle of iron grid with the access hole up through the middle of it. To stand up you needed to keep your feet on that curved shelf, away from the centre. The walls around it were no higher than waist height, with three sturdy metal poles supporting satellite antennae rising slightly above head height. Handing Lucky unceremoniously to the sheikh, Matt unclipped his harness from the ladder rope, hauled himself up through the access and stood next to Carra—up close and personal. There was no space for a third person; that was obvious. Matt glanced around, the wind whipping his face, and deliberately blurred out what lay beyond. Instead he found himself staring, with wonder, at the graffiti. Not many people had been here and most of them, it seemed, had left their mark . . . *M Qasem, Divicca, Bazi, Gecko,* and, incongruously, *Jo McNally.* He felt an odd compulsion to fish a felt tip out of his pocket and scribble: *Matt Wheeler was here at the end of the world.*

Instead he said: 'Carra—we can't all fit. You can see that.'

'Not in here,' she said. 'But you could all go over the edge.'

'What?!' Matt gaped at her.

'She's right,' came a voice from below. Hazza, holding Lucky on one fist, stared up at them. 'The harnesses you're wearing are for abseilers. All the connections are up there. It's designed for it. You *can* hold hands and connect to Carra—give her the boost—just as long as you're hanging outside the crow's nest.'

Matt felt his knees give way.

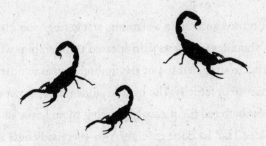

CHAPTER 31

It took so much yelling and bashing to get people to move. Spin was on to house number five before he saw the first family emerge, running, from the end of terrace which lay closest to the quarry cliff face.

Holding what looked like a double duvet over their heads, the mum, dad, and two kids began to run along the pavement. He recognized the man as the first whose door he had pounded on. 'Don't look back!' the dad yelled. 'Just keep moving!'

A rumble above them made the kids scream but they kept on running—so they did not see their home caved in by a lump of chalk and limestone the size of a minibus.

Spin found himself standing, staring in disbelief for a few seconds, before several other families whose doors he'd beaten just a minute earlier charged past him.

'Come ON!' yelled one of the mums, staring at him. 'GO! GO!'

Spin turned and ran in a slanting, staggering lope, clasping his right shoulder tighter as pain speared through him with every step. He struggled to put the umbrella up as another hailstorm rose in ferocity. The handle juddered in his fist as ice marbles battered the parasol, wreaking more havoc in his shoulder. Had he done enough? Was everybody out? As house two and three and four began to collapse under further avalanches, Spin could see the dust rising further along the cliff face—the part that hung over the industrial estate. Velma was a red blur, pelting along its perimeter wall.

But surely nobody would be working there this early? After the storms and the hail?

Better hope not. First one and then two warehouses were pulverized as a massive slab of cliff face slid down onto them, its network of weeds waving cheerily as it descended. Clouds of chalk and lime dust were pluming up through the hail. How far could the avalanche travel, he wondered? Could it reach the perimeter? Could it flatten the metal fence and roll out across the access road, wiping out the families now fleeing along it?

Maybe not . . . but it *was* travelling. It was time to get out of here. He'd done his good deed for the day.

He ran alongside the families, keeping pace now, despite the grinding pain in his shoulder. The hail, mercifully, converted to heavy rain. Spin pictured himself at home, lying down in his shady basement room, still and calm, breathing away the pain. Soon he would be there. That was the thing to focus on now.

Home. Dark, still, and calm.

Velma cut across his path, nearly tripping him. The idiot animal ran *towards* the perimeter and slid sinuously through a gap in it. Where the *hell* did she think she was going? Spin peered out from under his dented black parasol and groaned aloud as she stared back at him, tail high, whiskers twitching.

No. No no no *no*. He was NOT a hero. He was NOT.

And yet here he was, running across the access road and heading for the gate into Quarry End . . . or what was left of Quarry End. More than half of it was now a steaming stew of chalk and limestone and shale . . . the guts of the old hill spilling across the land that had been brutally carved from it centuries before. The warehouses, offices, and cabins closer to the outer fence were still visible and on one of them—right up on the *roof*—stood a solitary figure. It was a man in a dark uniform. A security guard. Even from here, Spin recognized him as the young guy who manned the booth beside the gates into the estate.

He should be running for his life but no—for some insane reason, instead he was standing on the roof of a cabin, clinging to an old aerial, and staring his doom right in the face. Behind him was only a three metre drop onto grass, but he was mesmerized in front of the collapsing cliff.

Spin ran for the cabin. On any normal night, without daylight smashing him in the face in the form of a white water deluge, without a messed up shoulder, without an interfering fox forcing him to *Do The Right Thing*, Spin could shin up onto that roof in a matter of seconds.

This time it was going to be harder. Unless he *refused* to believe in the pain. It had to be gone. It had to not matter. He flung the broken brolly aside and made his limbs do exactly what they would do on any normal night, in the dark. He launched himself up to the roof, boosting his trajectory with a hard kick off a small generator at the back of the cabin. He swung his legs across the flat, rain-soaked surface, toppled the guy, and rolled him, screaming, off the edge, to the grassy patch below. Then he leapt down after him, landing hard with a jolt that might well have permanently disconnected his arm.

As the avalanche rumbled across the sky above him, the only other thing he could do was drag the dazed security guard beneath the cabin with him. It was the last thing, too, it turned out. A second later Quarry End cliff sank to its knees, bent over, and kissed every living thing in its path goodnight.

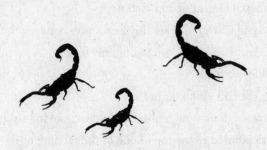

CHAPTER 32

'How lucky that you're an expert in abseiling!' chirruped Elena, through chattering teeth. Not *good* luck, obviously, she thought, as Hazza checked all her metal connections. Some other kind of luck.

Already hanging off the crow's nest of the tallest tower in the world, were her two best friends. They were quiet; at least she couldn't *hear* any whimpering past the droning of the wind. Even Lucky, told firmly by Matt to stay *inside* the spire, clung to the uppermost rung of the ladder and stared up at her in silence. Elena felt her hair whip past her face. It was a good thing she had a helmet on or it would be *such* a mess! She gave a hysterical giggle. The fact that she might wet herself at any moment ought to be more of a concern.

'I can come out too,' said Hazza, addressing Carra who was

sitting up on the rim of this tin mug in the sky, to allow space for the sheikh to gear up her victims.

'No,' said Carra. 'You are the connection between the circuit and me. And I will need you to hold my feet.'

'Hold your feet?'

'Yes. When I climb higher.'

'Carra . . . there *is* no higher!' he argued, looking stunned.

Carra pointed to the top of one of the satellite boxes.

'You're not serious!' said Elena. 'Tell her she's not serious!' she said to Hazza.

'You can stand on the wall of the crow's nest, if you really have to,' he said. 'I will hold your feet. And you'll be strapped on.'

'No,' said Carra. 'I must—'

'Just hold on a moment!' said Hazza. 'Let me get Elena over the edge and then we will work this out.'

Elena felt something inside her simply collapse with terror. She couldn't do this. She couldn't. She *couldn't*.

'It's OK,' called a small, quavering voice. Tima was attempting a smile as she hung over an incomprehensible drop. 'Just do what he says. It's easy . . . really.'

'Put your feet flat against the spire,' said Hazza. 'And lean back against the ropes. Put your feet wide . . . make a triangle. Don't look down.'

Stepping over the edge nearly burst her heart. She thought she might faint and her limbs seemed to dissolve with panic. All she could do was stare, terrified, into the steady brown eyes of the man who was pushing her off the Burj Khalifa. *He's an expert. He's an expert. He's an expert*, she chanted to herself. *He knows what he's doing. You're safe.*

She clung to the taut rope, stretching from her harness to a strong metal ring on the edge of the spire, closing her eyes and praying that this would all stop *right now*; that it would do the decent thing and be a **NIGHTMARE**. Not reality. She just could not do this. And then she reminded herself that eleven-year-old Tima was already doing it. And so was Matt—both of them on either side of her, making a circle around the spire; making Carra's circuit. Without a third Night Speaker to complete the circle, it wouldn't work – they couldn't reach each other. She had no choice.

'Lean back,' said Hazza. 'Kick away a little and let your feet find the surface.'

She did as she was told and felt the solid metal connect with the soles of her trainers. She dared to open her eyes and glance to her right. Matt gave her a rigid grin.

Back in the crow's nest, Carra was arguing with Hazza.

'The signal will be scattered by all this metal on me,' she was saying. 'It can be *around* me, but it cannot be on me.'

'Carra . . .' Hazza sounded aghast. 'You *cannot* stand on a tiny satellite box on the top of this spire in a force five wind . . . with no harness.'

'You will be my harness,' said Carra.

'But if you slip and I only have your *feet* . . .'

'The simple answer you need to give me is yes,' said Carra. 'Because we are running out of time.'

'So you keep saying, but—'

'Look to the west.'

Elena, in spite of her rictus of terror, creaked her head around to look west, across the city and out into the Persian Gulf.

On the horizon was a massive, billowing black cloud.

The mother of all sand storms was coming.

'What will you do if they save the world?' asked Callie, as they sat on the blue leather sofa like a pair of tourists. 'Will you stay on for a bit?'

'I don't know,' said Steve. 'I could see a few more sights maybe.'

'Will you be in trouble with the PM for not showing up?'

'Not when everyone learns what I came here for,' he said. 'Will Elena be in trouble for skipping school?'

'No . . . it's the Easter break now. We'll have to go right back though, because I've got no money left—and Matt's on parole. I took a chance and booked returns for tonight. We can sleep on the plane . . . although it won't be easy in economy seats.'

'If your daughter and her friends manage to save the world,' he said. 'I will be paying for you all to go business class.'

'Really? I didn't think scientists made *that* much money,' she said, laughing.

'They don't . . . I'll be billing the Prime Minister.' He sounded more chipper than he felt. In truth, he felt like one of the musicians on the Titanic; resignedly playing on as the ship sank. He'd had a text through from Chase in Virginia with the latest figures on the planet's slowing spin. It was exactly as they'd predicted. It was going to get more catastrophic by the day . . . the hour, even. Once everyone understood, the end of civilization might well arrive by the weekend.

But there *was* a chance. What was all this for if there wasn't?

Callie suddenly let out a very unladylike word and stood up.

Steve looked outside and let out some ungentlemanly words of his own.

The horizon had gone from serene hazy blue to a bubbling mountain of dark cloud.

'Another sandstorm!' Callie shook her head in horror. 'Look at it!'

The first one had been bad enough—but it had blown through in just a few minutes. This one was a monster—three times the height and density.

'They might have already done Carra's communication thing,' said Steve, trying for optimism. 'They could be coming down right now. It's been nearly an hour.'

Callie nodded, looking dazed with worry. He gave her a hug. 'It's OK,' he said. 'That Hazza chap really sounds like he knows what he's doing. I'm sure he'll keep them out of danger.'

Tima decided to watch Elena hanging onto the edge of the crow's nest rather than look behind her. If a killer storm was on its way, she didn't want to look it in the eye. Looking *up* wasn't too soothing, either. Carra was climbing the satellite connection box—a tall, rectangular canister of metal which jutted into the sky a little higher up. Just when you thought terrifying had no more meaning for you, Carra showed you a whole new dimension.

She had bullied the sheikh into allowing it. She had slipped out of her harness, pulled a long, wand-like metal device out of her bag, tucked it into her zipped up jacket, and climbed up without a moment's hesitation.

The top of the satellite box was flat . . . and no bigger than a shoebox in surface area. Rising next to it was a thin bronze pole with what looked like a pear drop on the top of it . . . a small decorative Arabian offering to the heavens. Carra took a hold of it and used it to help her stand.

With no harness.

Hazza stood on the rim of the crow's nest—a foot anchored on either side of its iron circle—and grabbed Carra's ankles with both hands as she plucked the metal wand from her jacket. Her long dark plait buffeted her face as the wind rose around her. She softened her knees, crouching lower for a better centre of gravity, to manage the gusts.

Then she let go of her handhold to tweak something on the device. Tima stifled a scream as Carra swayed there, fiddling until some blue lights lit up along its side. Then, with a sudden, heart-stopping sway to the left, Carra snatched hold of the bronze post and steadied herself. Even Hazza cried out then, and swore eloquently in Arabic.

'MATT!' cried Carra, as soon as she'd regained her balance. 'I need you to take off your shoe and put your foot against Hazza's leg.'

Matt nodded and adjusted his angle so he could lift one foot away from the metal barrel of the crow's nest. Elena and Tima instinctively put out one hand to steady him, just managing to reach each of his shoulders. Letting go of their ropes even with one hand was unthinkable—but it had to be done.

Matt hauled his left trainer off and tried to throw it into the crow's nest—but a gust of wind blew it back again, narrowly missing his head. In the corner of her eye, Tima watched it spin away into oblivion—and hoped nobody was standing beneath it when it reached ground level. At terminal velocity it would probably knock them out cold. Matt wasted no time looking down but stretched his foot across to where the sheikh stood on the rim, and hooked his toes around the man's ankle.

'Now link hands . . . all of you!' yelled down Carra, her voice snatched away by the wind almost before it could be heard.

This was the most heart-stopping moment. The moment when Tima had to let the rope go completely, and trust that it would hold her safe in the harness. Her left hand slid down Matt's arm and found his hand and, finally, finally, she forced her fingers to uncurl from their death grip on the rope and reach a shaking right hand across to Elena. Their fingers swiped the air for a few panicky moments, then found each other and grabbed on for dear life.

This had better work, Tima told herself as the back of her neck began to sting. *This had SOOO better work!*

'Are we all connected!' yelled Carra, turning her face to the east to avoid the thickening blast of sand.

'YEESSS!' everyone bellowed.

And Carra clicked something on her device. It pulsed blue and then green and then red and Tima thought she could hear a high-pitched note amid the increasing shriek of the sandstorm.

After a few seconds Carra called down: 'I have sent the message!'

'Can we get back in again?' begged Tima. 'Can we?'

'No,' said Carra.

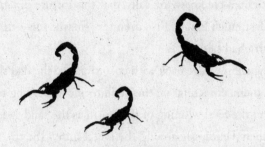

CHAPTER 33

What day was it now? Matt had no idea. Most of his existence was taken up with keeping a grip on the hands of his two best friends. Best *human* friends. He was so glad his best bird friend wasn't out here. Lucky would have been swept away.

To take his mind off the unshakeable reality that he and Elena and Tima were being sandblasted at 828 metres, he forced his thoughts back to Thornleigh. What was Mum doing now? Was she cooking lazanki? It was Matt's favourite of all his mother's Polish dishes—pasta with chopped fried cabbage, pork, onion, and mushrooms. Yes . . . he could see her cooking it now, and singing one of her funny Polish songs. Dad was out. Everything was warm and calm. Ben was home on leave and they were playing a bit of retro Spyro together while they waited for dinner.

A vicious blast of sand stung his cheek and he screwed his eyes up tighter. He knew, logically, that this torture *would* end. It couldn't last much longer. Five minutes—maybe ten—that was what Carra had said.

'They will message back with co-ordinates,' she had shouted down to them, crouching on the satellite and struggling to be heard over the feral whining of the storm as the sand-laden wind slithered endlessly around the metal spire. 'The co-ordinates will tell me where to aim to create the solar flare. I must get the angle right and I will need another boost from you all. You must stay where you are. It won't be long.'

It was long.

It was longer than his whole life.

What day was it? He had no idea. Probably the day when he needed to show up for more litter picking. There was no way he was going to make that date. The boss would report his absence and when they arrived home he would be arrested, returned to court, and then sent to a young offenders' institution. But why worry about that? Time had obviously stopped. Or he had died and been sent to hell for all the bullying he'd done before he met Elena and Tima. He was going to be dangling from a skyscraper with one freezing cold foot and 60mph grit eating into his face until the end of time.

Tima wished she wouldn't cry. It wasn't *proper* crying . . . her eyes were just leaking. She couldn't open them for even a second; the sand would get in. The wind carrying it was cold around her body now; it was hard to imagine they were in the desert. When would this end? Her brain did a freaky little flip, imagining undoing the boiler suit and pulling her mobile phone out of her jeans pocket for a quick flick through her texts to while away the minutes. Her inner workings bunched up tighter (was that even *possible?*) as she imagined the endless queue of texts from her distraught parents. Maybe she deserved this fate; maybe she would die up here because she'd been such a bad daughter and caused them so much pain.

She would give anything to be back with them now. If the world was going to end, she should be with them. Back home, having tea, playing with Spencer in her room. But maybe that's what she would give up . . . Spencer and all the other spiders and the insects too. Maybe she could give up her Night Speaker power and get a normal life back for everyone. Would she? Could she?

A huge gust sent her lurching sideways and Elena and Matt grabbed hard at her hands, holding her against the spire. She knew they would never let her go. She could never let them go, either.

It was something, at least, that Mum was downstairs with Steve. Elena was barely hanging on now. She was in a world of stinging pain and terror and the only small comfort was that her mother was not here to see it. If Elena died up here today—and this was looking increasingly likely—she guessed the scientist would look after her mum. They had seemed to click on the plane journey and during the escape into the desert, talking easily about pretty much everything; laughing at each other's jokes. For however long the human race had left, she thought Steve would be there for Callie.

Tima—so light compared to the rest of them—was suddenly blown sideways, breaking Elena out of her bleak reverie as she gripped down hard on her friend's hand to pull her back to the spire. As Tima's feet thudded against the curved metal, Elena heard Hazza yell: 'We have to get them in! It's too rough out there! Too dangerous!'

He and Carra were huddled back inside the crow's nest. Carra had climbed down to wait for the response from her people. She had made it clear that there was no time—or space—for the rest of them to get inside too, and still be able to get out again and make another circuit for the solar flare attempt.

'I know!' yelled back Carra sounding uncharacteristically wretched. 'I *know*. It is a terrible thing they must do!'

'I can't let this go on!' bawled Hazza, getting up and reaching for the rope that Tima was suspended on.

And then she heard Carra scream: 'IT'S HERE! I HAVE THE RETURN MESSAGE! I HAVE THE CO-ORDINATES!'

'DON'T TAKE US BACK IN!' shouted Matt, his eyes tightly closed and his face averted from the worst of the sandblast. 'FINISH THE JOB!'

Carra didn't need telling; she was already climbing back up.

'This is INSANE!' cried Hazza. 'You have to wait for the storm to die down!'

'The co-ordinates will be useless in five minutes!' Carra

yelled back. 'They are calculated for the orientation of the Earth and moon and sun NOW!'

Hazza gave up arguing. He leapt up on the rim of the crow's nest and grabbed Carra's feet once again as she teetered on top of her tiny metal shelf. Through the swirling brown vortex of sand, Elena made out the shape of her, crouched, head down into the wind, one hand gripping the bronze pole and the other pulling the communicator out again. Of course, it wasn't *just* a communicator—it was an intergalactic weapon of immeasurable power; the size of a torch—probably more powerful than NASA's entire resources put together.

Matt hooked his foot around Hazza's ankle once more and the three of them clenched their hands together even tighter, completing the circuit.

Carra was keying into the device with one thumb. Her body was convulsing; Elena realized she was coughing again. Coughing a *lot*. But she was unstoppable, because a moment later she was standing tall, lifting the device—like the Statue of Liberty; holding aloft what was very likely mankind's last hope.

And then ... she dropped it.

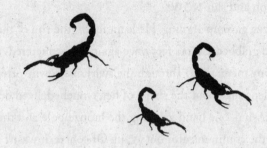

CHAPTER 34

Mankind's last hope spun past Matt's head in slow motion, end over tip over end over tip, like a trapeze artist, still blinking red, green, and blue.

He let go of Elena and Tima and threw himself backwards to catch it and it actually rebounded off his little finger as it fell. Matt's mouth opened to allow a cry of deep, deep rage and pain to flood out of his throat as he tipped backwards, losing his connection with the spire and flipping over so his head was hanging down and his wide, appalled eyes could properly watch the communicator fall.

The cry wouldn't stop. He just shrieked and shrieked. It no longer mattered where he was or who he was or how much sand was flying into his eyes, nose, and mouth. All that had ever mattered was that bit of alien tech which was now plummeting to earth. That was it; the very thing his whole fifteen years of existence had been rushing towards—this moment when human life on Earth survived or ended. He was here to help but he'd blown it and now all he could do was witness all hope ending and there was nothing left of him at all but skin and bone and shrieking.

Eventually a silence overtook him as he dangled. No sound at all. Just the image of the twinkling lights vanishing into the dust cloud. Then nothing. Nothing. Nothing.

Lights.

Lights again. They were still in view. How?

They were getting closer. How?

The movement was jerky. It took him several seconds to understand why. The device was not magically levitating back to Carra—it was being carried.

Matt's eyes bulged and his forehead pounded as his blood rushed to his brain. It was an eagle; one of the three who had guided them this morning had followed them here. It had *caught* the device as it fell and now it was climbing, wings beating with immense effort through the spinning vortex of air and sand, and rising, rising, rising . . .

At last it skimmed past his face, a wing feather actually brushing his nose, and on up to Carra, who had been crouched, frozen in horror, on her perch. The eagle flew up past her, letting out a screech of triumph as it dropped the device into her hand. Carra caught it and yelled: 'MATT! GET BACK UP! NOW!'

Matt scrabbled at his rope and tipped himself upright again. He could barely see anything; his eyes were full of sand and his head was swimming. But he felt his hands grabbed by Elena and Tima and his feet reconnected with the metal. He put out his shoeless foot, found Hazza's ankle, hooked around it and prayed to the beam that it wasn't too late.

Ten seconds later the whole spire began to hum with a deep, singing vibration and a needle-thin red laser shot up into the sky.

Beside him he heard Elena sing in a thin, cracked voice: 'You are my sunshine . . . my only sunshine . . . you make me happy . . . when skies are grey . . .'

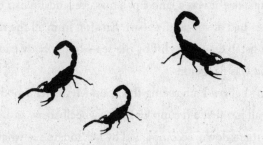

CHAPTER 35

The people of Thornleigh were digging with spades, forks, tin trays, and bare hands. Nobody knew how many people might be buried under the avalanche but some said at least two were under it—the security guard who'd been up on the roof of the cabin and the young man in black who'd leapt up and dragged him underneath it just before the rocks and dust engulfed them. They feared there might have been some early shift workers in Castle Ironworks too.

Everybody from the terraces was accounted for—and some of them were here, digging. Digging and pausing and listening for sounds of life. Fire and rescue crews were coming with sniffer dogs but nobody was willing to wait.

Mrs Patel from the pharmacy thought it was the kind of scene you might see after an earthquake . . . but she had never expected to see an earthquake in Thornleigh. Some said it wasn't an earthquake—it was a landslip; a massive landslip like they sometimes had down on the coast. Erosion from all the rain had made it unstable—like a cliff by the sea—but nobody had ever thought it was dangerous.

'I can't believe I am seeing this,' said Mrs Patel, who had emptied all her first aid supplies into a wheelbarrow and wheeled them down, accompanied by her son, to see what they could do to help. So far it had been minor injuries—cuts and bruises and one suspected broken wrist. She was glad the ambulance was making its way through the ice and the floods for the poor souls under what was left of the Quarry End cliff. She could do nothing for them.

'It must be climate change,' said Mohammed. 'It wasn't supposed to happen this fast, though.'

A woman wrapped up in a black trench coat, black headscarf, and black gloves stepped up beside them. 'Have you seen a boy?' she asked. 'Tall—fair hair—wearing black. Kind of vampire-y . . . ?'

'There was a boy who got everyone out of the terraces before the cliff fell,' said Mohammed. 'He was tall and wearing black—but he's—' He stopped short when his mother's elbow connected with his ribs.

'Nobody knows for sure where he went,' said Mrs Patel, touching the woman's gloved hand. 'But if it's your boy—he's a hero.'

'That doesn't sound like my boy at *all*,' said the woman with a dry chuckle, but she squeezed Mrs Patel's hand back again.

'This is so scary,' said Mrs Patel. 'It's happening all over the world—freak weather; earthquakes; volcanoes.' The other woman nodded but didn't speak. Her face, shadowed by the headscarf, looked pink and stressed in the morning light. 'Well, at least the rain has stopped and the sun is coming out,' said Mrs Patel, reaching for anything positive on this terrible day.

The woman in black just groaned, turned around, and hurried away.

'Wow . . . look at that,' said Mohammed. 'What's that all about?'

On the other side of the fence a fox was picking its way across the mess of rock and debris, pausing and sniffing every now and then, in full view of everyone.

'Maybe she's lost her cubs,' said Mrs Patel. 'Poor thing.' Briefly she wondered about Elena Hickson—the young carer whose mother had bipolar. One evening last week, she had spotted Elena walking on the edge of the woods, apparently in company with a fox very like this one. There was something very unusual about that girl. Hopefully she and her mother were safely at home today and not caught up in anything like this.

It was a terrible day for Thornleigh—worse even than when the power station caught fire and exploded and then there was a swarm of wasps. Worse than the week when there was a massive undetected gas leak and everyone was falling ill and several people with weak lungs or hearts ended up dead. She really hoped this was the final bit of horror for her town. She'd had quite enough.

A watery sun washed the sky a hopeful blue—you could see

the three quarter moon still up over the western horizon.

Then the sky turned red and everyone started screaming.

CHAPTER 36

In the IERS hub, Dr Chase Hamner leapt to his feet and yelled: 'Oh my god, oh my god, oh my *god!*' in a very unscientific way. 'Did you see that? Did you *see it?*'

The cacophony around him convinced him that everyone had. 'Solar flare! A massive solar flare!' screamed someone. 'We've got sputtering off the scale!'

'Satellites are down!' yelled another one. Some of the screens went blank but not all—their systems were designed to battle on through the occasional effects of solar flares.

The screen in front of Chase was working just fine, and the image on it—a live feed from the International Space Station— was taking his breath away. Not just the reach of the mass of plasma thrown out by the sun, but the way it was organized, almost as if it was *directed*. And if so, it had been directed at the moon.

The ejection had struck the satellite's exosphere and something . . . *something* . . . was spinning away from it. Chase gaped, trying to crush the enormity of what he was seeing into his brain, like a python trying to swallow a cow. Baxendale's Jodrell Bank contact was *right*—there WAS something on the dark side of the moon.

But not any more. The kick back of plasma and rock from the moon's surface had evidently destroyed it.

He put his head down in his hands for a while, slowing his breathing.

'Europe is freaking out,' called out someone who was monitoring news.

'Big red sky event!'

Chase's fingers rippled across his keyboard. He was still staring at the fresh calculations, five minutes later, as he picked up the phone and called Baxendale. The phone went to voicemail so he left a message: 'Steve . . . the sun just whupped the moon and your lady at Jodrell Bank might like to know that something *was* hiding on the dark side. It's now a cloud of space debris. This could be the solution to our slow down problem. I'm really hoping so. Call me!'

He put down the phone and said to everyone: 'OK—time to tell the world what that was, before people start throwing nukes at each other.'

CHAPTER 37

They were dragged in, one by one, by Carra and Hazza. The sand stuck to Tima's skin like plaster, clinging to the layer of cold sweat her terror had produced. But if she thought she could finally rest, she was wrong. There was no room to rest.

Hazza hauled her into the crow's nest, detached her abseiling lines, and then reattached the guide rope for the ladder inside the spire. She sagged in his arms and he gave her a little hug before commanding: 'You can't give up now, Tima. You have to be strong a while longer. I need you to climb down inside—all the way, as quickly as you can. You can rest at the bottom.'

Her arms and legs were quaking with exhaustion and fear, but she knew he was right. She had to make room so they could rescue Elena and Matt. She climbed down and found Lucky waiting on the top rung, anxiously peering up for her boy.

'He'll be here soon,' she said, stroking the starling's head with trembling fingers. Lucky flitted across to the other ladder to allow Tima to descend. There was no way the bird was going anywhere without Matt.

Tima took a deep breath and began to climb down, sternly telling herself to get a grip—literally—and to keep moving. Above her she could hear Elena murmuring in shocked relief as she was pulled inside the crow's nest. Was this over? Could they really believe it?

Stop thinking—keep climbing, she told herself. Down, down, down for what seemed like hours. A couple of minutes above her, Elena was also descending on the opposite ladder. Tima wanted to call up to her but couldn't spare the energy. At last her feet landed on the floor of the inner spire. She crumpled to the concrete and began to sob with relief and when Elena arrived she did the same, before dragging Tima into a tight hug. 'We did it . . . we did it,' she gasped out, between hitching breaths and gulps.

Matt arrived three minutes later, with Lucky flapping around his head as he sank to his knees. He didn't cry but his face was slack with exhaustion, beneath its sand and sweat mask. He ran a hand through his hair and red-brown dust showered out of it.

Carra arrived next, looking as wrecked as the rest of them. And finally, the sheikh, sand in his beard and a rather shell-shocked look in his eyes, leaning back against the rungs and letting out a long exhalation before sinking to his knees.

There was very little space but they all ended up on the floor in a heap of burnt-out humanity. For a minute or two they just breathed and glanced at each other. At long last Matt sat up straight and croaked: 'Tell me it worked.'

Carra pulled the communicator/laser/bringer of solar flares gadget from her jacket and held it out. There was an orange light blinking on its end, which seemed to please her. 'The co-ordinates were correct and the laser reached the target; the part of the sun's surface closest to the dark side of your moon—and the Ayotian vessel hiding there. The disruption will have triggered a powerful solar flare.'

'Has it wiped those Ayotians out?' asked Matt.

'I cannot tell you this,' said Carra. She paused to cough. 'But we will know soon.'

'We need water,' said Hazza. 'We must go down.'

Everyone got awkwardly to their feet in the tight space, and then stepped out onto the small platform at the base of the spire. Sunshine greeted them; the sandstorm was now just a dark cloud on the eastern horizon. Three greater spotted eagles and one scops owl greeted them too, all four perched on the glass and chrome balcony. Matt stepped closer and one of the eagles bent its beak towards him. 'Thank you,' he breathed and the eagle made a low grunting noise in response. Did it know what it had just done? What the human race owed to it?

Hazza cried out in wonder. 'How do you *do* this?' he said. 'I fly falcons but they are reared and trained by me—these birds are wild!'

'It's a long story,' said Matt, stroking the eagle's fierce, beautiful face. 'It's OK—she'll let you.' And the eagle did allow the sheikh to touch its feathers and marvel.

'You can tell me the story,' said Hazza, 'after you have bathed and rested. I have an apartment here, a few floors down.'

'Oh yes,' moaned Tima. 'Yes, yes, yes. Bagsy I go first in the bathroom.'

'You may all go first,' said Hazza. 'There are six bathrooms.'

CHAPTER 38

Matt lay deep in sweet-scented bubbles and watched the plasma screen TV through the glass wall of his bathroom. The hot water soothed his body but the images on the screen were slowly soothing his mind. Although the sound was off, CNN was showing—with text scrolling along the crawler at the base of the screen.

Eclipsing the last forty-eight hours of freak weather events was the Red Sky Over Europe story. For nearly two minutes, roughly an hour ago, the sky had turned deep red. The light show—shared on screen in viewers' shaky mobile phone films—wasn't steady. It drifted in waves reminiscent of the aurora borealis—the northern lights, but in the south too, and the east and the west. The sight had amazed and terrified millions from Norway to Spain, from Greece to Ireland.

But the freak events—the abnormal tides, earthquakes, storms, and undersea volcanoes—had all subsided. And along the bottom of the screen crawled some reassuring words from the planet's top scientists:

NASA confirms Earth narrowly missed by undetected meteor . . . once in a millennium event now safely past . . . massive solar flare is result of close call with ½ km space rock . . . freak weather events now settling . . . 976 believed dead across the world in past 36 hours . . . climate change not main cause . . .

Much of what he was reading he already knew—even the meteor cover story. Twenty minutes earlier, while Matt's bath was running and he was downing a pint of water and stuffing baklava in the massive reception room of Hazza's apartment, Steve had been hatching the meteor story with his American scientist mate.

'It'll be scary,' Steve had agreed, talking earnestly into his mobile phone while he walked up and down the marble floor past the most breathtaking view in the kingdom. 'But not as scary as an intergalactic warship full of hostile aliens parked on the moon. I will give you and your NASA mates a full briefing the day after tomorrow. No—not before. NASA will have to wait until I've got back to London and briefed the Prime Minister. Also, I have some people to get home.'

Matt had hit the tub at that point, retiring to his private

guest suite on what was actually Hazza's entire *two floors* of the Burj Khalifa. Elena and Tima were probably doing the same thing right now, lying back and soaking away the terror of the past couple of hours. Even Carra had agreed she could do with a shower, although she did not seem as shaken as the rest of them. But then, she was a marshal for this 'quorat' of planets she kept talking about. She'd seen a lot of action on her journeys around the cosmos. Today was probably business as usual for her.

As his insides slowly unknotted and sleep began to call to him, the natural state of his everyday concerns began to pop up to the surface, like unsinkable rubber ducks.

Mum. Dad. His reparation order . . .

'NO!' he said, aloud, creating a small tidal wave of hot water and foam as he stamped his feet at the far end of the tub. 'Just give me a *break*.'

'A break!' echoed Lucky, from her perch on the solid gold tap and shower arrangement.

Hazza's staff had arrived at his private apartment minutes after they'd all stumbled into it, and magically produced food, drink, bathrobes, towels. The sheikh had told Matt, Elena, Tima, and Carra to rest for at least a couple of hours while he spoke to Steve and Callie and made plans. What plans? Matt was too tired to wonder what plans.

All their secrets had unravelled with the arrival of that Ayotian ship; Elena had told her mum the full truth, Tima had texted the beginnings of the truth to her parents (who were to be collected by Hazza's drivers and brought here by teatime)— and he . . . he had left Mum and Dad in no doubt that he was involved in something deeply suspicious. They probably thought he was in a criminal gang.

He knew he should call Mum but he was so, so tired. He would probably just cry—and that would really scare her. He'd allowed Callie to send Mum a text, saying he was safe and he would call her later . . . but only once he was safely in his room and not available to deal with the response.

No. He had to sleep before he made a single other decision. He got out of the luxurious bath before he could nod off and drown himself in it. Then, dried by a huge, fluffy white towel, he slid between the silk sheets of a king-size bed, pressed the remote control button that closed the floor-to-ceiling curtains, and dropped his head on the pillows. Lulled by the sighing of the air conditioning, he dropped into a dreamless sleep.

Elena badly wanted a bath but she was too tired. She got into the shower instead, washed the sand from her skin and hair, towelled herself dry, and dropped into the fabulous silky bed. She didn't even close the curtains before she hit the pillow.

Crashing into dreamland was just the escape she needed from the trauma of the last couple of hours . . . but her mind wasn't ready to let her go. Since becoming a Night Speaker she had encountered a demonic underworld god, killer plants, interplanetary child kidnappers, and monstrous earth-drilling grubs . . . but in truth she had never known true fear until she'd climbed off the top of the Burj Khalifa.

The calculations weren't through yet but Steve was pretty sure the Earth was back to spinning at the correct speed. Even two seconds out of sync had thrown up horrific results and hundreds of people had died around the world.

Did she dare to believe it was all over? From deep inside her, a tremble began . . . turning to a shake and then a non-stop juddering throughout her frame. She understood what it was . . . aftershock. She lay and shook, her teeth chattering, for several minutes . . . until her body could take no more and finally lay still.

And then she slept.

It had been, Steve reflected, *one hell of a week*. This time last week he was mooching around with fellow lecturers at the university, trying to win the hearts and minds of scruffy undergraduates and pursuing his research project on the northward spread of warm water marine life. The most exciting thing that ever happened was an occasional guest slot on BBC Radio 4.

Now, here he was in a private miniature palace half a kilometre above the Arabian Desert, discussing how to handle the recent defeat of an alien attack force with one of Dubai's most eminent sheikhs. And that wasn't what was worrying him.

'These kids,' he said, keeping his voice low because Callie was now snoozing, under a blanket, on a golden velvet sofa near the window. 'I need to protect them.'

Hazza nodded, sipping on some hot, sweet coffee. 'They are exceptional. Imagine what they can do . . . communicating with other species . . . controlling the animal world.'

'It's not control,' said Steve. 'It's collaboration. They've been at some pains to point that out to me. If it was only control, then the camels and the scorpions and the raptors would never have sought them out and taken them to *you*—possibly the only man in the country who could get them up the tower in time, no questions asked.'

Hazza nodded. 'I am honoured that they came to me. As far as I am concerned, they have earned the right to keep their secret, if that is what they wish.'

'I don't know how long they'll stay anonymous anyway,' said Steve. 'It's bound to get out but I hope, at least for the next few years while they're still growing up, that they can live as normal a life as possible. That's going to be fairly easy for Elena—Callie is ready to deal with it. Tima's parents? I don't know. But they are loving and decent and I'm sure they'll come to terms with it.'

'But the boy? Matt?' Hazza raised his dark eyebrows intuitively. 'Not so good?'

'According to Callie, his father beats him and his mother is too scared to protect him. He is worked hard, cleaning cars at the family valeting business at all hours. He was in court last week and got a suspended sentence for taking a car and driving it underage.'

'He is a tearaway?' Hazza looked surprised.

'Not at all,' Steve said, hastily. 'He was on a rescue mission—he had no choice! But, of course, he could not easily explain himself to the police. So he stayed silent and took his punishment.'

The sheikh nodded, thoughtfully, but before he could say

anything one of his men came to whisper in his ear. 'Tima's parents are here,' he told Steve. 'This should be interesting . . .'

Tima woke and wondered if this was a dream. The bed, with its silk sheets and gossamer-light duvet, was heavenly. As she sat up she realized her clothes—her stretchy black jeans and white sweatshirt, and her underwear and socks, were all washed, dried, and folded on a footstool.

She got dressed and slipped out to find the others, but before she entered the grand reception room she heard familiar voices that rooted her to the spot. *Mum and Dad! HERE!*

'This is all very hard to believe,' her father was saying.

'Are you sure you're not mistaken?' said her mother.

Tima took a deep breath. This was going to be a very difficult conversation. But before she could step into the room a woman dressed in blue robes approached her, carrying a small bamboo cage. 'His Royal Highness said you might need these,' she said, smiling.

Tima took the cage, thrilled. Inside it were twenty or more butterflies—beautiful blue, red, and violet wings shimmered across a cluster of twigs and green leaves. She closed her eyes for a moment, picturing how it would go. This was a dream . . . a fantasy she had been acting out in her head for nearly a year now. Because if she had to spell out the truth to her parents, at least she could spell it out with butterflies . . .

CHAPTER 39

They all flew home first class, courtesy of Hazza. Tima and her parents—who were wearing an almost permanent expression of confused wonder—were seated ahead of Matt. Elena and Callie were behind.

Steve and Carra were closest to him. Each of them had their own little pod of luxury, with seats that became beds at the touch of a button, widescreen TVs, a tiny minibar with drinks and snacks to one side, a blanket, slippers, headphones for watching movies, unless you preferred to stare at the view from cameras mounted on and under the plane. It was head-spinning stuff for Matt. Three hours into their flight, Steve quietly told them all that his friend in the IERS had texted to confirm the Earth was now back at its normal rotational speed. Carra, looking pale and tired, smiled as they all whispered their thanks to her. 'Couldn't have done it without you,' she said.

After an exquisite meal served with silver cutlery and thick cotton napkins—and plenty of Champagne for those old enough to drink it—they all slept, on and off, for the rest of the flight, but Matt was roused several times by Carra coughing. Lucky, perched in a bamboo cage close to the window (the airline would only take her on board because of the personal intervention of the sheikh) copied the cough and said '*Help!*'

Matt pushed his velvety blanket aside and padded the short distance down the thickly carpeted aisle to Carra's pod. He found her taking her inhaler, dragging the drug inside it deep into her lungs. After she'd finished she looked up at him and smiled thinly. She looked pale and there was a faint wheeze to her breathing.

'Carra,' he said quietly, kneeling next to her. 'How long can you really stay on Earth? I mean . . . it doesn't seem like your inhaler is working too well.'

Carra nodded. 'My lung capacity is reducing,' she said, as if she was discussing a faulty car engine. 'I calculate I have less than an Earth day left to live.'

'What?!' hissed Matt, a familiar sense of dread leaping back into his throat.

'Do not worry,' said Carra. 'I know how to find the corridor cave. And now the Ayotian ship is gone, my exit will not be blocked. I will return to Targa in time to recover.'

'We'll come with you,' said Matt. 'All of us. To be sure you make it through.'

'That is not necessary,' began Carra.

'No, it's not,' cut in Matt. 'But it's the right thing to do. There's no way we're not coming.'

Carra gave him a genuine smile. 'You are a fine human being, Matteus Wheeler.'

There was no delay in landing this time; all air traffic control was back to normal—but as they flew low over the southeast coast, on approach to Stansted Airport, the extent of the flooding was clear. Huge swathes of the coast were dappled with inland lakes, which could pass for natural if you didn't look close enough to see the many roofs dotted through them. Hundreds of homes had been drowned and the water was taking its time to recede.

The plane landed on time, just after 7 p.m., and coasted to its gate. First class passengers swept past everyone else, with their priority cards; leaving Matt feeling oddly ill at ease as he carried Lucky through in her bamboo cage. Except it wasn't odd at all. He was an imposter in this world—he didn't belong in such luxury; he was a downtown kid with downtown prospects. Or at least, that's what he'd always expected to be. Maybe everything had changed now. Even if, as planned, they did not reveal their secrets to the wider world and kept on going to school as usual, living their lives much as before . . . things *were* different now. His life was never going to be normal. It might even . . . it might be good.

Elena and Tima caught up with him, the lone figure with no family here except a starling, and linked their arms in his. 'We're going to take Carra to the corridor cave as soon as we get back,' said Elena. 'Just us. Mum and Steve have agreed—and Mum's working on Tima's parents right now.'

'I keep *telling* them,' said Tima, rolling her eyes, 'with my Night Speaker powers they never need to worry about me again!'

'You're their little princess,' said Matt, gruffly. 'They're always going to worry about you.'

Priority cards swept them right past all the queues at passport control and as they stepped up to the barriers with their passports at the ready, Matt began to feel himself getting more grounded. The planet was revolving as it should and everything was getting back to normal.

Tima and her family went through first, then Elena and Callie. Carra glided through all the security monitors without so much as a beep, thanks to the baffler in her backpack. Nobody queried the solar-flare-inducing gadget hidden inside.

Matt hung back, worried about Lucky, but the guards on the first class priority card gate had obviously been briefed, because they just motioned him through, still carrying the cage. Nothing beeped. They were home.

Steve followed and then the party made their way through the arrivals hall, stopping to allow Tima and her parents to collect their cases. As the electric doors slid open to reveal the exit plaza, Matt undid the door on the cage and let Lucky fly. She did a couple of low arcs under the high ceiling and then headed for his shoulder.

But before she could get there a heavy hand fell upon it. Matt jumped and spun around.

'Matteus Wheeler,' said the police officer. 'Please come with us. You're under arrest.'

CHAPTER 40

'This can't be happening!' Elena groaned, as they watched the police officer press Matt down, hand on his head, into the back seat of the patrol car.

Everybody had protested—everybody had tried to stop Matt being taken away, but the officer only got highly defensive and then two armed airport police showed up, hands resting on their weapons, backing up their colleague from the Norfolk Constabulary.

'Leave it,' Steve had said. 'We can't fight this battle today.'

But they could at least follow Matt. The patrol car was alongside the taxi rank. Steve hailed a large people carrier with enough seats for them all, and they got inside. 'Follow that police car,' said Steve, with obvious relish. 'Don't let it out of your sight.'

'Well, that's a new one,' said the cabbie. 'Do you know where it's going?'

'Probably Thornleigh in Norfolk.'

'Won't be cheap,' said the cabbie.

'It's fine,' said Steve, holding up a wallet stuffed with credit cards. 'I can cover it.'

Elena wondered how on earth they would have managed without Steve. Where would they be today if she hadn't gatecrashed his lecture last Saturday? Hazza had paid for their flight back, but Steve had covered everything else in Dubai and the desert. After so long managing on their own, it was an incredible relief to have backup from adults with resources.

'Quick!' yelled Tima. 'They're getting away!'

Elena almost laughed, Tima was so theatrical, but the situation was too awful. After everything he had been through— all that he'd risked to save the planet—Matt was once again going to get punished while the rest of them got away with it. It was always Matt who put himself on the line and got nothing back for it but trouble. It was so deeply unfair.

'Lucky is following the car too,' said Callie. 'See—that's her isn't it?'

'Yes,' said Elena. 'Brave little bird.' The starling had refused to fly back into the cage which Matt had handed to her, preferring to fly after him instead. While everyone had been shouting at Matt's arrest, Lucky too had been yelling 'No! No!' as she dive-bombed towards the man cuffing Matt's hands behind his back.

Matt had called out: 'Lucky! Stop! Fly home!' just before she landed on the police officer's face, angry beak and claws at the ready.

Now she was coasting along above them as the patrol car turned out of the airport and headed north.

'How are we going to get him released?' asked Tima, looking tearful. 'He couldn't get back for his youth offender team meeting this morning, so that means they'll send him to prison, doesn't it? I can't believe they've arrested him already!'

'I think maybe they found out he'd left the country without his parents' permission,' said Callie. 'They might have decided he was up to no good. They must have put him on a watch list. They would have known when he was coming back as soon as his named cropped up on the ticket booking.'

Steve was texting madly on his phone. 'I'll see what strings I can pull,' he said.

The patrol car wasn't in a hurry; no blue flashing lights went off and it followed the speed limit steadily on the M11. Elena became aware that Carra was no longer sitting up, watching the road ahead. She had slumped into the corner of the car and was resting her cheek against the window. She didn't look well and her chest was hitching every few seconds. Elena leaned across and said 'Use your inhaler again!' Carra's dazed eyes refocused; she sat up and did as Elena suggested. 'Is it helping?' Elena asked. Carra nodded and smiled thinly.

She wasn't fooling anyone.

'We need to get Carra back to the corridor cave,' said Elena. 'I hate to say it, but we might have to leave Matt where he is for a while—we have to get Carra home.'

'Don't worry. I have ...' Carra consulted the gadget on her wrist. At the touch of her finger it sent up a small hologram, which appeared to display her vital signs in graph form. '... three hours and twenty-seven minutes before I expire.'

Everyone stared at her in horror and Tima's mother leant over and took her pulse, frowning. 'We should get you to hospital—now,' she said.

'Your hospital could not save me,' said Carra. 'I can live on your world for several days if I expend only normal levels of energy ... but ...'

'... you just climbed up the tallest tower in the world and harnessed the sun to save humanity,' finished Steve. 'Thank you, by the way.'

Carra nodded and closed her eyes again. Elena checked her watch. It was 8.30 p.m. and the light was fading fast. They had to get Carra to the other side of Leigh Hill. Matt would understand—it wasn't something they could delay.

But as the car took the exit into Thornleigh twenty minutes later, it was obvious that nobody was going anywhere fast. Queues of traffic snaked into the town past closed lanes on the A road where rows of fire engines and ambulances were parked.

'What the hell ... ?' murmured Elena.

'Oh my god!' said Tima, who was on her phone, looking at the local BBC news site. 'Oh my *god*!'

Everyone leaned in to read the headline Tima was waving around: **SEVERAL FEARED DEAD IN THORNLEIGH HILL COLLAPSE.**

'Oh no,' breathed Elena, suddenly prickling with dread.

'What happened?'

Tima read aloud: 'A Norfolk town is in shock today after a hillside collapsed onto houses and an industrial estate. The town was hit by a deluge of rain and hail on an unprecedented scale before the quarried cliff face of chalk and limestone collapsed, burying homes and businesses around breakfast time today.'

She looked up at them, gulping, and then read on as the taxi inched through the slow traffic just behind the police patrol car carrying Matt.

'Locals say the death toll would have run into scores of people if a local teenager hadn't knocked on doors and warned everyone to evacuate, less than a minute before the first avalanche,' Tima read on. 'Families fled a terrace directly beneath the cliff with seconds to spare.'

Elena felt the prickling sensation intensify. 'Who was the teenager?' she asked.

'"He definitely saved our lives," said dad of three, James Cardell whose home was destroyed. "It was raining so hard, with so much hail, that we wouldn't have heard the cliff starting to come down. This lad dressed all in black came and smashed on everyone's doors and yelled at us to get out. We got out only just in time."'

Tima raised her eyes to Elena's. Elena *knew*. She just *knew*. 'Spin,' she said. Tima didn't argue.

As if it had been planned, their taxi turned the bend on the narrowed road and suddenly the whole scene lay before them, beyond a line of emergency vehicles and *DO NOT CROSS* tape, bathed in emergency lighting as darkness crept across the eastern sky. Teams of rescuers were working across rubble which appeared to have engulfed most of the buildings in Quarry End.

Carra began to cough, dragging their attention away from the shocking view. It was a horrible, hacking cough and the way she was sucking in the air between each spasm was frightening. 'We have to get her over the other side of Leigh Hill,' said Tima. 'Me and Elena know the way to go.'

'We'll come with you,' said Steve. 'We may need to carry her.'

'No,' grunted Carra. 'Night Speakers only.'

'But you're sick—you need help to get there!' said Callie. 'We can't drive you—the road doesn't go around that side of the hill.'

'Night Speakers . . . *only*,' insisted Carra. 'Get . . . Matt . . . back.'

Elena peered through the windscreen. From here she could see the back of Matt's head as he sat on the rear seat of the patrol car. *How* could they get him back? He was so desperately needed. The traffic was at a standstill. Elena bashed on the back of the cabbie's headrest. 'STOP! We need to get out!'

The cabbie put on the brakes, peering over his shoulder, perplexed. 'I can't park here, love,' he said. 'There's nowhere to pull over.'

'It's OK—three of us are getting out. That's all!'

'Wait!' said Tima's mum and dad, in panicked unison.

Tima grabbed their hands and said: 'You *HAVE* to let me go. *Trust* me! I will be back. I will be safe.'

'Trust them both,' urged Callie. 'We have to let them go.'

And they did. They sat back in their seats, looking dazed,

and they let their little girl jump out of the taxi with her friend and their alien ally.

Outside the traffic was at crawling pace. Elena and Tima took an arm on either side of Carra and walked her along beside the patrol car. Above them, Lucky was flying in agitated loops. Matt glanced out through the window and widened his eyes as he saw them. He didn't move but he looked up to where the starling circled, picked out by emergency arc lighting set up across the disaster zone.

'We need help, Lucky!' called up Elena. 'We have to get Matt out. You know what to do.'

Lucky soared up into the sky and for a few seconds they kept pace with the cars which were nudging along at walking pace.

'Tima . . . can you do your thing?' asked Elena.

'Waaaay ahead of you,' said Tima. A dark, glittering cloud was already forming above trees to the west of the wrecked industrial estate. The insects funnelled down through the air in a whispering tornado as they made right for the police patrol car. They smothered its windscreen. The patrol car windows were closed but it was only a matter of seconds before the flies, wasps, bees, moths, and beetles found their way in through the ventilation slots.

There was panic inside; the doors were flung open and the driver and the officer who'd arrested Matt leapt out onto the road. Matt gave a shout and the officer flung his door open and pulled him outside too. The insects swarmed the men's faces but kept a respectful distance from Matt. He grinned at Elena,

Tima, and Carra, and tried to run to them, but the officer, even with a swarm around his face, was dutifully hanging on to his prisoner.

Tima didn't want to ask the wasps to sting, but she was just getting ready to do it when the birds arrived. Onlookers might have thought the gulls were there to pick off the insects, but not one of them snapped up a snack. The insects, sensing their shift was over, spiralled back up into the air and evaporated into the night while the feathered relief crew mobbed the two beleaguered officers.

However professional he was, Matt's arresting officer could not keep a hold of his prisoner while he was being dive-bombed by a thirty-strong flock of gulls. With a shout of alarm, he threw both hands up to protect his face while his colleague dropped to the road and curled up in a ball.

Matt charged towards his friends, and ran with them along the dusty edge of the road, Lucky flying close behind him while the gulls continued to hold the police officers down. They sprinted through the trees on the industrial estate perimeter and then followed the woodland paths they knew so well from their nightly wanderings.

Matt had, thankfully, been uncuffed during his journey in the patrol car. He and Elena grabbed hold of Carra and supported her as they moved swiftly through the dark wood and began to climb the hill. Their alien friend was incredibly determined but her strength was failing fast. As they reached the top of the hill she sank to her knees, dropped onto her hands, and arched her back, desperately pulling in air through her weakened lungs.

'Oh god,' wailed Tima. 'She can't go on. We have to carry her.'

Matt and Elena hoisted Carra up, pulled her arms across their shoulders, while Tima grabbed her feet, holding them on either side of her waist and pulling ahead. It was slow going and the strained wheezing noises Carra was making were terrifying.

'We're not going to make it in time,' Elena moaned. 'We're not!'

She became aware of motion around her and realized that they had company. Lots of company. There were four or five foxes, three badgers, and two small deer. As they staggered along the animals pushed in around them and to her amazement, Elena felt the burden of Carra lift. The two small, sturdy deer had both ducked beneath Carra's sagging back and boosted her up on their strong shoulders. The foxes and badgers pushed in close too, staying in step. With no hands free for torch bearing, this was crucial—there was no need to pause and seek out the right path; the animals were guiding them.

The journey down the hill was fast—faster than they could ever have managed alone. They might have spent many precious minutes trying to navigate back to the old well, but there was no need; their animal friends had it all covered.

As soon as they reached the spot they put Carra gently on the ground. Elena and Tima took out their torches; Matt's was still in his backpack in the patrol car. They had replaced the well cover when they'd rescued Carra, but they hadn't hammered all the nails in. Elena had felt guilty about it at the time, in case anyone stumbled upon the wooden cover, pulled it up and fell down the well.

Happily, nobody had—and it was a good thing they'd been left, because there was no time for pulling out nails.

They flipped up the cover and shone their torches down. The well shaft had rungs set into its side, not unlike those in the Burj Khalifa (Elena shivered as she thought of it)—but of much older, blackened metal.

Carra seemed to have roused herself. 'I can do it,' she said, between wheezes. 'It's not so far.'

'We're coming with you,' said Matt. 'No arguments.'

'Fine,' said Carra, with a weak smile. 'No arguments.'

CHAPTER 41

Matt went first, reasoning that he was the biggest and so best able to cope if Carra fell on him. Carra didn't seem as if she would fall, though. She seemed to be squeezing all of her remaining energy into a bunch and *making* herself move. Above her was Tima, and Elena came through last. Lucky flapped up and down between them all as they descended. The journey down the well was dark and muggy but nothing compared to the epic climb down the spire of the Burj.

A metre or two above a flat black circle of water Matt found a ragged hole in the brick leading away into a tunnel through the rock. 'This way?' he called up, flashing the torch Tima had lent him.

'Yes,' said Carra. 'You will need to crawl.'

Once inside the tunnel, which was cramped and damp,

Carra activated something on her wrist gadget which sent a lilac light in all directions, making their journey a little easier. Matt expected to be crawling for hours, remembering the state Carra had been in when they'd found her—but it emerged that the main reason she had been so exhausted was that she'd spent several hours digging carefully through rock falls to find her way through to the well. Her efforts were paying off for them all now, as they simply clambered through the gaps she'd made.

At last they reached a part of the tunnel big enough for them to stand up in. 'We are in the old exit point,' puffed Carra, getting to her feet. She pointed to a rockfall off to her right, in which lay some massive chunks of limestone, way too heavy for one person to lift. 'That is why I had to find an alternative route,' she explained. 'Come . . . this way.'

They turned a corner and all let out an exhalation of wonder. The corridor cave was pure white, circular, and smooth like marble. In its centre was a hexagonal plinth of white rock with a small hexagonal post, no taller than a pencil, set into it. A steady beam of golden light streamed from the post into the wall of the cave, at a slight upward angle.

'This is what connects to the corridor cave in Scotland,' murmured Tima—'where the beam begins and ends.'

'Yes,' said Carra. 'And it's where my journey begins and ends.'

'Did you make it like this?' marvelled Elena. 'So smooth and beautiful . . . ?'

'Sometimes creating a corridor makes heat—a lot of heat,' said Carra. 'If you heat chalk and limestone enough it becomes marble.'

'You're feeling better, aren't you?' said Matt, watching Carra's face regain some of its colour. Here in the centre of this pearl, she looked more beautiful than he'd ever seen her.

'The beam cave will always make me feel better, but it is not enough to heal my lungs,' said Carra. 'I must go now. Thank you for getting me here.'

'Thank *us?!*' spluttered Tima. 'We have to thank *you!* You put your life on the line for everyone on Earth—again!' She flung her arms around Carra. 'I totally forgive you for planning to kill me that time,' she said.

Carra staggered back slightly, looking bemused, as Tima finally let her go. She shouldered her bag of alien tech and knelt by the hexagonal post. At once it began to shine out sparkles of pink light, like a twinkling dandelion clock, dancing around the white walls and reflecting in her eyes. 'You know, don't you, that nobody else can ever come here?' she said.

They nodded.

'I wanted you—and you only—to see this place,' she went on. 'You have all earned the right to see it. Once I am through to the other side it would probably be wise to blast back through the corridor until this cave collapses,' she said. They all looked aghast. 'But I think I will leave it here, just in case. I don't think I will see you again—there are many other planets to protect.'

Matt felt his throat tighten. It was hard to believe they'd never see her again.

'But you must all vow—to me here, now— never to come back here.'

Matt gulped; it was a hard thing to promise. 'Not even if the world starts falling apart again?' he asked.

'Well,' said Carra, with a smile. 'Maybe then. But not for fun. Not for curiosity. Do not tell your parents or Steve where it is. They will be too tempted. Do not make a path to this place because one day someone might follow you who has no business being here.'

'How will we contact you if something else happens?' asked Elena.

Carra thought for a moment. 'The odds of something like this happening again in your lifetime are vanishingly small.'

'Yeah—but . . . even so,' said Elena. 'Will the communication stick work again?'

'Yes,' said Carra. 'If I'm still around to answer it. The life of a Quorat marshal can be short. I don't think you'll use it again, but keep it somewhere safe.'

Tima put out her hand. 'Come on everyone—hands together,' she said. Elena put her palm down on Tima's and Matt added his. Lucky landed on top of it.

'I promise,' said Tima.

'I promise,' said Elena.

'I promise,' said Matt.

'I promise,' said Lucky.

'It has been . . . most interesting,' said Carra, smiling. Then she turned away into a column of green light and stepped into another dimension.

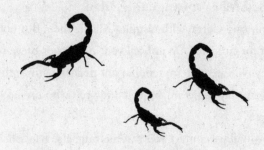

CHAPTER 42

Matt let himself into the flat in the early hours. He'd sent Lucky back to her roost with her family of starlings hours ago, as soon as they'd climbed out of the well and nailed the cover back down, using a bit of flint as a makeshift hammer. His feathered friend badly needed to rest and recuperate.

He and Elena had walked Tima home first. She'd given them a tearful hug and then the door had burst open and light flooded out as her parents stood there, looking wrecked with relief.

'Lots of talking to do before bed,' Tima had sighed. 'See you both tomorrow, I hope.' Then she'd run into the tearful embrace of her mum and dad.

He and Elena had walked back to hers in near silence; both too tired and emotional to say much at all. Callie had flung the door open in a very similar way to Tima's parents. The warmth that flew out to meet his two friends was tangible.

'Matt, love,' said Callie, sending a little of that warmth his way. 'Why don't you stop over with us? I can text your mum and say you'll be back in the morning?'

Matt shook his head. 'Nah. Better go now. No point putting it off.'

Elena hugged him then. 'You can stay with us any time you need to,' she said. 'Seriously. Mum's about ready to adopt you.'

'Thanks,' said Matt. 'I'll bear that in mind.'

Now, as he stood in the darkened landing of the flat, he wondered if he *should* have taken up Callie's offer. One more night away from Dad might have been wise. He glanced at the door, remembering the padlock and was surprised to find it was gone. The marks left by the screws were evident but there was no sign of all that metalwork. Odd.

The flat felt different. Unusual. He wandered into the kitchen and found washing up in the sink and the remains of takeaway pizza on the table. He frowned, puzzled. Mum *never* left the kitchen like this; she was very tidy and insisted on leaving everything clean and neat before going to bed.

The sitting room was a mess too, with beer cans left on the coffee table and the sports pages of The Mirror strewn across the sofa. Maybe Mum had finally gone on strike and told Dad to clear up after himself.

He sighed and took himself off to bed. He was way too tired to think about any of this. In his room, where everything looked much the same apart from the emergency escape ladder flung angrily across the carpet, he slumped onto his bed and took off the new, very expensive pair of trainers, brought to him by Hazza's staff in Dubai yesterday. He had no idea where his old, missing trainer had landed. It was probably bobbing around in the ornamental lake at the base of the Burj Khalifa, occasionally surfing on the spectacular fountains.

He flopped back on his bed, too tired even to undress, and began to drift away.

The next thing he knew, a dark figure was standing over him.

'You,' it said. 'It's *your* fault.'

Matt shot up, heart thudding.

His father reeked of alcohol and sweat as he switched on the overhead light, revealing that he looked no better than he smelled—unshaven and crumpled, in a stained vest and boxer shorts.

'Dad—I—' The words were knocked out of him as his father grabbed him by his sweatshirt and dragged him up off the bed.

'You snivelling, lying, cheating waste of space!' he spat, and threw his son against the wall. 'It's thanks to you—all of this is thanks to you. She's gone because of you!' He cracked his palm across Matt's jaw and it felt like a whiplash.

Dad staggered back, wiping perspiration off his face, then came in for another blow.

Matt shot his right arm up and deflected the blow with a strength that shocked him. His father staggered backwards, stunned. Matt had only done this once before and he guessed his dad had decided that was a one-time thing. Well it wasn't.

Dad didn't back off like last time. With a roar of rage, he

came at Matt again and this time Matt blocked his right fist and grabbed his left and twisted it, exactly as Spin had taught him. His father was wrenched sideways and toppled heavily onto Matt's bed with a cry of shock.

A split-second image of Spin sprawling on the deck of the bandstand came to him. *'Come on, then! I'm down but I'll be up again in a second if you don't disable me!'*

He leapt forward, pinned back Dad's flailing arms and put his knee on the man's damp, clammy chest. Then he leant close to the shocked face and hissed: 'ENOUGH! Do you understand me? I have had ENOUGH!'

He was ready for more—for cursing and struggling; even spit in the face.

What his father did next was far worse.

Dad crumpled beneath him and began to cry.

Appalled, Matt stood up, letting him go. Even now he wondered whether this was just a ruse and he was about to get headbutted. But no. His father just curled up, sideways, like a baby, and began to sob.

Matt stood over him, horrified. He should be feeling triumphant . . . but he didn't. He felt terrible. His father's face, flabby and puckered and wet with tears, was an awful thing to see. Matt's treacherous mind threw up memories of Dad at Christmas, giving him a present to unwrap with happy excitement. Back when he was younger; back before the drinking really started. Back when he loved him.

Matt found he was crying too. Not because he hated his dad, but because he still loved him. That was the awful kicker.

The very worst thing; loving someone who seemed to want to destroy you.

Matt stood, tears flowing down his face, hands at his side, and wondered what the hell to do.

On his bedside clock, the digital figures clicked over from 1.33 a.m. to 1.34 a.m. The beam came sweeping through. Matt could see it. *Really* see it. The golden light coursed through the room and the song filled his heart and soul the way it always did . . . and this time he almost detected a scattering of beam light dropping onto the man weeping on his bed.

Matt sat down, dragged his father up into a sitting position, and wrapped his arms around him.

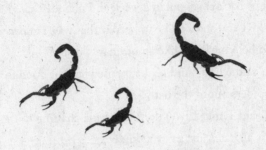

CHAPTER 43

Conversation over breakfast was . . . awkward. Mum and Dad were still processing everything that had happened over the past couple of days. Tima wasn't sure exactly how they were feeling about learning the truth. They were being weirdly . . . polite.

'Would you like pancakes?' Mum said, smiling brightly. 'With syrup . . . and berries?'

'That sounds like a lovely breakfast,' said Dad, also smiling brightly and fiddling with the salt and pepper pots.

'Mum—Dad,' said Tima. 'Stop being weird. I'm still me.'

They glanced at each other and it was clear they'd been talking about how to manage this situation. Operation 'let's be normal' really wasn't working. Mum sighed and sat down at the table. 'We . . . we just don't really quite know . . .'

'. . . what to do . . .' went on Dad.

'Don't do anything!' said Tima. 'Just be like you've always been. I'll be back at school in a week and nobody there knows how freaky I am, and I'd like to keep it that way. I'm *depending* on you to help me seem like an ordinary person!'

'OK,' said Mum. 'And . . . I suppose you'll be good for getting spiders out of the bath . . .'

'Yes,' said Tima. 'If you don't mind me chatting to them. Spencer is a *friend*, just so's you know.'

'You could be pretty useful in my practice too,' said Mum, looking thoughtful now, and even a little excited. 'I mean . . . there is no vet in the world that can *ask* their patient what's wrong . . . but with you around . . .'

'You see! There are loads of positives!' Tima grinned. 'Yes please to pancakes!'

There was a buzz in her pocket and she plucked out her phone. There was a text from a number she didn't recognize. She could see Elena had also been sent the message:

Handing myself in today. Not sure what's going to happen. Have asked Dad to let you know. This is his phone. Matt.

She gaped at it in disbelief, before texting, at supersonic speed:

When are you going in? And where?

She wanted to add:

AND WHAT THE HELL?!! YOUR DAD'S PHONE?!! HAS HE JUST BEATEN YOU TO A PULP?!!!

But obviously, if it was his dad's phone, his dad would see it.

Going into Thornleigh Police Station around midday with Dad. Wanted to let you know in case I don't see you for a while.

Before Tima could deploy her fast thumbs, Elena's text response appeared:

WAIT for us outside. We'll be there!

No need, he texted back.

NEED! Tima shot back, just before her phone rang.

'We need to make some calls,' Elena said.

CHAPTER 44

Matt's mum had left the day he'd taken his passport and escaped through the window. She had told her husband of twenty years that she'd had enough and there was no longer any point trying to make it work. She'd really only stayed with him for Matt and Ben's sake and now it was clear that she'd made a big mistake. She should have *left* him for Matt and Ben's sake.

Dad told him this over a cup of strong coffee and buttered toast in the kitchen. He'd tried to tell him in the early hours but he'd not made a lot of sense as he cried himself into exhaustion and in the end Matt had laid him down, curled the duvet over him, and let him sleep. He'd cleared the sofa for himself and snoozed a bit there.

'She's definitely gone, then?' Matt asked, eating a bowl of Cheerios and milk. 'It wasn't just for a few days?'

'She's gone.' His dad's eyes welled up and he sniffed deeply. 'And I don't blame her. I don't blame you or Ben either. I'm a crap dad.'

Matt didn't argue. 'Maybe if you stop drinking she'll come back,' he said, after a pause.

Dad looked at him, his eyes bloodshot, and nodded slowly. 'Maybe,' he said.

Matt knew he couldn't avoid the Young Offenders Team issue. As he and Dad cleared up the kitchen he said he was going to hand himself in. He didn't tell Dad anything about where he'd been and Dad didn't ask—but he said he would come with him. He said it in a way that sounded OK. Supportive.

Lending Matt his mobile to text Elena and Tima was eerily kind and, in truth, Matt didn't trust this new state of affairs. The truce between him and his old man was a very fragile thing.

Handing himself in wasn't dramatic. He'd half expected the desk sergeant to leap across the desk and get him into an armlock, but in fact all that happened was he was asked to fill in some forms and then taken away to a holding cell while his Dad sat on a bench and waited. There'd been an awful lot going on in Thornleigh that week; his small violation wasn't big news.

A duty solicitor was called in to see him and arrived half an hour later; a short man with a lined face and a scuffed leather briefcase.

'So,' he said. 'Alleged breach of referral order. Can you explain to me, Matteus, why you were unable to attend your litter picking session on Wednesday?'

'Would it help if I said I was saving the planet?' said Matt.

'No,' said the duty solicitor. 'It wouldn't.'

There was a knock at the door and the desk sergeant came in, looking somewhat baffled. 'It's OK,' he said to the solicitor. 'Turns out you're not needed.'

'Really?' The solicitor got up, surprised, but still gathering his papers.

'Yup. Clerical error. He didn't miss his appointment after all.'

'Righty-ho,' said the solicitor and departed.

Matt walked back out to the public area, dazed. 'What . . . what just happened?' he murmured.

The sergeant looked at him appraisingly. 'Got a call from up the line—well above my pay grade,' he said, eyebrows raised. 'Seems you've got friends in high places. Your rap sheet is clean. Off you go—ideally before my colleagues who picked you up yesterday catch sight of you. They seem to think you brought down some kind of biblical plague upon them.'

A small crowd awaited him outside—his dad was having what looked like a fairly awkward conversation with Dr Stephen Baxendale, Callie, Elena, and Tima. Matt wandered across to them, adrift and confused.

'How did you do that?' he asked.

Steve waved his phone. 'I've got the direct line of the Prime Minster, don't you know? And after my briefing last night, the PM knows a certain young man is owed a favour or two.'

Matt gaped. 'The PM knows who I *am*?'

'Oh no,' said Steve. 'Your identity is still safe. I was given some temporary codes and passwords by the Home Office . . . to iron out a few things on your behalf. You don't need to clear any more litter. And you no longer have a criminal record.'

Matt shook his head, astonished.

'Also,' said Steve, 'Hazza's wondering how you might feel about spending some time at his place in the summer holidays, working with his birds of prey. He thinks even his best falcons could use a bit of extra training.'

Dad was looking absolutely baffled. Of course, he knew nothing about where his son had been or what he'd been doing.

'I'll talk it over with Mum,' Matt said, planning to get over to his aunt's house, where Mum had gone, right away. 'And . . . then me and Dad need to talk a bit more too.'

'Yeah,' said Dad. 'Yeah, we do.'

CHAPTER 45

It rained on the day of the funeral. The church wasn't as full as it might have been; Elena guessed he hadn't had many relatives. Maybe twenty people were there, sitting quietly in the pews, heads bowed, while the vicar spoke in front of a black lacquered coffin.

Spin would have loved that, she thought. If he could have been here to see it.

'Last week was something the people of Thornleigh will never forget,' said the vicar, casting his eyes gravely across the congregation. 'The whole world will not forget the catastrophic events caused by our near miss with the meteor. But Thornleigh's own catastrophe is what *we* will remember the most. For some that will be because there is a visible scar now, forever, on the edge of the town. We will be able to see what remains of the

Quarry End side of Leigh Hill for generations to come. But for others—for you, here today—it's the human cost that will stay with us. And here we are today to mourn a young life lost on that terrible morning.'

Elena saw a woman dressed in black lower her head. Spin's mother, she realized. She'd only seen her once before, but she still recognized her, even from behind.

Elena took a long slow breath and gulped away the tears which threatened to overwhelm her. Maybe she should have asked Tima and Matt to come with her today, to pay their respects, but she hadn't. She'd wanted to come on her own.

'Cris was a man full of life,' said the vicar. 'His mother tells me he preferred nights, which is why he was in Quarry End so early. Half an hour later and he would have gone home, but that wasn't to be.'

Spin, he'd once told her, *was the less boring end of Crispin.*

She drifted a little as the vicar went on, telling everyone how wonderful the dead young man was, as if he'd known him personally. Then they were all singing a hymn and she was burbling along with them '... *in our hearts, Lord, at the end of the day* ...' and then it was over. People made their way out of the church, dabbing tissues at their eyes and murmuring quietly about how lovely the service was. She could go and stand at the graveside if she wanted to but it seemed a bit much. She wasn't family, after all.

Instead she turned down an overgrown side path, which led away from the graveyard and back towards a cutway into the woods. It was dim and dark but she took some comfort from that. She guessed she might always be a creature of the night now.

'Elena?'

She turned around.

'You *are* Elena, aren't you?'

Spin's mother, holding a black umbrella, stepped closer to her. She looked pale, thin, and strained, but her eyes were a bright blue-green just like her son's. Her white blonde hair was just like his too.

'Sorry . . . it's a shame to meet you at a time like this,' said his mother. 'I'm Astrid, by the way.' She put out a gloved hand and Elena shook it.

'It is . . . so sad,' gulped Elena. What else could she say?

'I think he'd want you to know,' said Astrid, 'that . . . well, you're the only girl listed in his mobile. That means something, I think.'

'A mobile?' Elena repeated.

'Waste of money!' sighed Astrid, with a sad smile. 'Barely used in three years! But your number and name were in there . . . and I remember him talking about you once or twice.'

Elena gulped and looked at her feet. 'He was a hero, wasn't he?' she said. 'He saved all those people . . . all those families . . . little kids.'

'He'd hate to hear you say that,' said Astrid. 'It'd mess with his whole dark, brooding, antihero legend!'

'It is NOT a legend,' said a cool voice, right behind Elena. 'It's a *lifestyle* choice.'

Elena spun around, and gaped in shock. The words fought

in her chest for a few baffled seconds, and then erupted from her throat in a sob. 'SPIN! I thought you were DEAD!'

'Well I prefer *un*dead if we're talking about my look,' he said. He was struggling to hold the umbrella because he was on crutches. There was a massive red graze down on side of his face and stitches on his temple.

'For god's sake, Crispin—I told you to stay in the car!' said Astrid.

'It's raining, it's dark, I can stand it,' he said.

'We have porphyria,' said Astrid, to Elena. 'Blood disorder— it's why we can't be out in the day.'

'Yes . . . Spin said,' breathed Elena, feeling lightheaded. She hadn't known Spin's surname. She only knew his full *first* name was Crispin . . . so when she'd heard on the local radio that a young man called Chris Spencer, who'd died in the Quarry End collapse, was being buried today she'd . . . totally got hold of the wrong end of the stick.

'But I felt I should come today,' Astrid was continuing. 'For the poor young man who died in the ironworks. Spin and the security guard made it after they got under the cabin, and it was so awful to think of another mother whose son *didn't* come home.'

'So . . . why were you telling me about my number in Spin's phone?' murmured Elena, still dazed and confused and overwhelmed.

'Oh . . . because he's been stuck at home with a broken leg and a messed up shoulder and driving me *insane*,' said Astrid. 'He needs someone his own age to talk to. He really does. And I gather you and a couple of others sometimes meet up with him in the evenings.'

'Mother,' said Spin, rolling his eyes. 'I do **NOT** need you to organize a play date!'

Astrid gave Elena a bit of paper with an address and a rough map on it. 'For pity's sake, save me,' she said. 'Come over this evening—all of you—I'll get in pizza.'

'**PIZZA?**' howled Spin. 'Oh dear god!'

Elena laughed. And laughed some more. Pure relief and happiness welled up inside her for the first time in . . . months probably. Months.

'We'll be there!' she said. 'Me, Tima, and Matt. Seven-thirty?'

'A bit early for us,' said Astrid. 'Nine o'clock? When it's properly dark?'

'Done,' said Elena. She looked at Spin carefully, trying to work him out. He closed his eyes and sighed and then gave her his usual crooked, smirky smile.

'Tell Car-wash Boy he might have a chance at beating me in a fight while I'm on crutches,' he said. 'But not to bet on it.'

Elena beamed, shook her head in wonder, and began to walk down to the woodland path. 'I'll tell him,' she called, over her shoulder.

'And tell Tima I don't want any theatrical hugs!'

'I'll tell her,' she yelled, chuckling.

'And tell Velma she can have my pizza crusts if she promises not to bite me ever again!'

'You hear that?' said Elena as the fox slid out of the trees and fell into step with her. 'You're welcome too. But I won't make you promise not to bite him. You always need to be ready to nip back where that one's concerned . . .'

Velma made no comment but she flicked her tail in agreement.

The woods folded around them. Elena took her time, moving almost silently, like Spin. She texted Tima and Matt (via his dad's mobile), wiping away tears; feeling relief and joy wash over her skin and through her soul.

Spin is OK! I thought he was dead but he's alive! And his mum has invited us all over to his for pizza tonight!

OMG! Tima texted back, thirty seconds later. **That is SO unreal! Mum and Dad say you can pick me up at 8.30 p.m.!**

Then, a text, freakily, from Matt's dad:

Matt says he'll meet you at your place, Elena, at 8.15 p.m.

Mum wasn't too upset about Elena deserting her at dinnertime, even though she was cooking her best curry. She'd asked Steve to come over.

'I could put it off and ask him another time, when you're here,' she said, oh-so-airily.

'You're so *not* putting him off,' said Elena, grinning.

'Oh . . . OK then,' said Mum, blushing just a little.

Even though it was very early for Night Speakers, Elena felt something like normality stealing back across her life as she and Matt called for Tima and the three of them set off through the dark woods towards Spin's place, checking the location on the scrap of paper with a torch.

'Nice brooch,' Matt said.

Tima—not required to look like a cat burglar for a change—was wearing a soft white jacket. Spencer's eight black legs were anchored into the woolly material of her collar. 'Just as long as Lucky doesn't like the look of him too much,' she said.

'Lucky knows the rules,' said Matt, stroking the starling's dark head, just under his chin.

'How are things with your dad, Matt? Are you two OK?' asked Elena.

'Not sure,' said Matt. 'I think so. But I'm going to stay with Mum and my auntie until he's sorted out the drinking. He seems to want to, so...' He shrugged.

Velma slid out of the undergrowth to join the party, trotting comfortably alongside Elena, touching a cool nose to the curve of her palm.

For a few beats, none of them spoke. Up ahead, a wrought-iron gate opened up in a high, ivy-clad, red-brick wall and a dark figure stood in the moonlight.

'Are you quite sure about this?' he asked. 'I might never let you leave, you know . . .'

'Give it a rest, you sad Goth,' called a voice from the house.

'*Mother!*' sighed Spin. '*Honestly!*'

ALI SPARKES

NIGHT SPEAKERS

THE BATTLE
BETWEEN GOOD AND EVIL
STARTS AT 1:34 a.m . . .
EVERY NIGHT

Elena, Matt, and Tima wake up at exactly the same
time, every night. It's becoming too much to bear,
until they find each other. And then they discover
what else they share: they have the power to speak
any language; they can even communicate with
animals. And what they learn with this power has
the potential to change their lives forever . . .

ALI SPARKES

NIGHT RAIDERS

TAKE A DEEP BREATH...
AND HOLD IT

Since the 1.34 a.m. wake up calls began, Elena, Matt,
and Tima had all had the power to talk to animals,
birds and insects like no other human could. None
of them would ever trade that for a full eight hours
sleep. It was too amazing. But they'll need this power
more than ever as a mysterious figure threatens to
destroy everything . . .

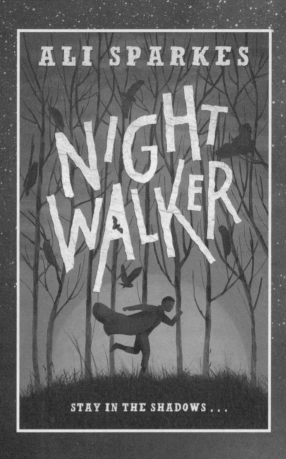

ALI SPARKES

NIGHT WALKER

STAY IN THE SHADOWS . . .

Something weird is going on at the hospital—
children are going in, and not coming out again.
Elena, Matt, and Tima are investigating, but even
they are struggling to uncover the truth. But Spin is
preparing to come out of the shadows, and when he
does, nothing will be the same . . .

ALI SPARKES

NIGHT TERRORS

SOMETHING LIES BENEATH.
AND IT BITES . . .

Deep underground, something is stirring.
Something huge and horrifying that has the
animals spinning in fear. And Tima is caught in
the middle of it. Can Matt and Elena get to her in
time? Something is going on below the surface,
and only the Night Speakers can stop us all from
falling into the cracks . . .

ACKNOWLEDGEMENTS

Night Forever might never have made it into your hands, dear reader, without the help of some marvellous people.

Huge thanks, then, to Jennifer Malton and Flora Rees of the Emirates Festival of Literature, for brilliant guidance in print and in person, on the details of life in Dubai—and the lowdown on the high rise of the Burj Khalifa.

Thanks also to legal goddess Natalie Rawson, for saving me from some embarrassing mistakes around the courts and sentencing procedures for young offenders.

And massive appreciation goes out to Dr Simon Boxall of the University of Southampton's School of Ocean and Earth Science for his vital guidance across this whole series—but most particularly in this story.

Nobody else could help me make the highly improbable seem quite so plausible . . .